Acting Edition

HAMLET, CHA CHA CHA!

Book, Music, and Lyrics by Monk Ferris

ISBN 978-0-573-68154-7

www.concordtheatricals.com
www.concordtheatricals.co.uk

MUSIC AND THIRD-PARTY MATERIALS USE NOTE

IMPORTANT BILLING AND CREDIT REQUIREMENTS

CAST OF CHARACTERS

HAMLET, Prince of Denmark
OPHELIA, his main squeeze
GERTRUDE, his mother, Queen of Denmark
CLAUDIUS, his uncle, King of Denmark
HORATIO, an amiable sponge
* [POLONIUS, Ophelia's father
  OSRIC, a court fop
* [GHOST, of King Hamlet the Late
  LAERTES, Ophelia's brother
ROSIE KRANTZ, Hamlet's school chum
GILDA STERN, his other school chum
CHORUS { THE TROUPERS, male singers/dancers
        { ELSINORITAS, female singers/dancers

*(the bracketed roles can be doubled)

[CHORUS members also do any other speaking parts, such as the Gravedigger, Major-Domo, Butler, Footman, etc.]

LOCALE: Castle Elsinore in Denmark
TIME: Roughly the 15th Century or so

MUSICAL NUMBERS

OVERTURE

ACT ONE

"BOO-HOO! I DO!" .... Gertrude, Claudius, Chorus
SEGUE #1 .... Rosie, Gilda
SEGUE #2 .... Rosie, Gilda, Hamlet
"THAT'S THE SPIRIT!" .... Hamlet, Ghost
"PRITHEE, BABY" .... Hamlet, Ophelia
"WHAT TO DO?!" .... Gertrude, Claudius, Polonius
SEGUE #3 .... Rosie, Gilda
"SOLILOQUY" .... Hamlet, Troupers
"GET THEE TO A NUNNERY!" .... Hamlet,
      Ophelia, Polonius, Claudius, Chorus
"TO BE SURE" .... Hamlet, Ophelia
"THE PLAY'S THE THING!" .... Hamlet,
           Ophelia, Chorus

ENTR'ACTE

ACT TWO

FANFARONADE .... Accompanist
"THE MURDER OF *THE MURDER OF GONZAGO*"
.... "Gertrude," "Claudius," "King Hamlet"
SEGUE #4 .... Rosie, Gilda
"HEEEEERE'S ROSEMARY!" .... Ophelia, Troupers
SEGUE #5 .... Rosie, Gilda
"DOWN, DOWN, DOWN!" .... Gertrude,
         Laertes, Elsinoritas
"YUCK! IT'S YORICK!" ...... Hamlet, Horatio, "Yorick"
"LET'S GET HIM!" .... Claudius, Laertes
FANFARONADE [reprise] .... Accompanist
"HAVE AT THEE *NOW*!" [#s 1, 2 & 3] ...... Accompanist
FINALE .... Company

[NOTE: Lest you be panicked by the profusion of musical numbers listed above, be it known that each SEGUE is but 15 seconds in duration. and FANFARONADE a mere 10 seconds]

"Hamlet, Cha–Cha–Cha!"

ACT ONE

Curtain rises on Castle Elsinore [see Stage Setting]; LIGHTING is bright and cheery, always, though on occasion (say, if play-action is only in areas F and D, only those areas should be lighted — but no matter what dire event is occurring, keep those lights cheery).

Re costuming: HAMLET wears only black; OPHELIA (except in her final outfit) wears white; everybody else should be in wildly bright colors, fuschia or chartreuse or cerise or glow-orange or whatever for maximal contrast with HAMLET's gloomy ambience.

At curtain-rise, OPHELIA enters via B, crossing toward C. She is short and very plump — but not fat — she's what the Germans call softich — all round and pink and rosy. Just as she reaches H, HORATIO enters via C, and they'll meet midway between H and I during:

OPHELIA. Oh, hi, Horatio! Have you seen Hamlet?

HORATIO. Not since the funeral. He didn't stick around for the wedding.

OPHELIA. Maybe he's sulking in the garden. I'll go have a look. (*continues toward C, but stops for:*)

HORATIO. Can you help me find the buffet table? Elsinore's such a *big* place, I can't find *anything!*

OPHELIA. (*gestures vaguely toward B*) There are at least *six* of them in *that* general direction! Just follow the sound of chewing.

HORATIO. Thanks, Ophelia! (*she exits via C; he starts toward B, but stops as HAMLET enters via B, looking solemn and sorrowful and weary*) Oh, *there* you are, Hammy! Ophelia's looking for you. She went *that* way.

HAMLET. Sweet and lovely maiden!

HORATIO. Who, me?

HAMLET. Jest not with me, friend Horatio, for lo I am sick and heavy of heart.

HORATIO. Too much pastry. It'll do it every time. Now if you'll excuse me, I have a date with some *Shrimp Louie!* (*starts to pass, but HAMLET takes his arm*)

HAMLET. So swift must you depart? Ages has it been since mine eyes have fallen upon thee!

HORATIO. (*impatient to depart*) So come along and *nosh* with me!

HAMLET. Alas, to feast would be to join in the general celebration of my mother's wedding, and to this laudation I can lend myself not!

HORATIO. But she's such a *pretty* bride!

HAMLET. *Ah*, the agony you do inflict upon me with that word! To be wed to mine uncle at the burial of her husband, my father, the late king! Her bereaved widowhood did persist not more than a handful of moments beyond my father's cremation!

HORATIO. Yeah, but think of all the money she saved on the church-rental!

HAMLET. (*cups an ear*) Hark! Do I not hear the approach of the bereaved woman even now?

HORATIO. (*cups an ear in same direction*) Sure sounds like *somebody* is headed this way!

(*HAMLET and HORATIO will move to area between B and G, looking upstage as MUSIC INTROS, and then CLAUDIUS, GERTRUDE and COURT [all the Ladies-in-waiting and Courtiers] come romping gaily in via A, with CLAUDIUS and GERTRUDE taking stances standing before their individual thrones, and remaining there, surrounded by happy COURT for duration of song. [NOTE: As brightly as they are dressed, CLAUDIUS and GERTRUDE each have a black mourning band upon the arm.] INTRO climaxes and:*)

GERTRUDE. (*sings*)
THOUGH I'M DEEP IN DEVASTATION
AT THE PASSING OF MY MATE,
I'M ALREADY BURNING BRIDGES TO THE PAST!
  COURTIERS.
HERE COMES THE BRIDE!
  CLAUDIUS.
SO, BY WAY OF CONSOLATION
LET US SWIFTLY CELEBRATE!
MAY OUR WEDDING TURN ALL GLOOM INTO A
  BLAST!
  COURT.
WE'LL TAKE IT IN STRIDE! [*will sing* "AHHH!"

now-and-again under.]
GERTRUDE/CLAUDIUS.
FROM MOURNERS TO LOVERS
WE'VE CHANGED IN ONE DAY!
THE SAD HEART DISCOVERS
THAT LOVE WILL ALWAYS FIND A WAY!

SO, WITH NO HESITATION
LET US DRINK TO HAPPY FATE
AS OUR HEADY YEARNING VOWS OUR LOVE
  WILL LAST!
  ALL.
THE FUNERAL HAD STREWN A LULL
UPON THE PATH TO BLISS,
BUT WEDDING BELLS PORTEND
HAPPY END TO THIS!
  GERTRUDE.
MATRIMONY'S RATHER SUDDEN
WHEN ONE'S NOT WIDOWED VERY LONG!
  CLAUDIUS.
BUT WHY DENY OUR HEARTS ARE THUDDIN'
TO LOVE'S SWEET SONG?
  GERTRUDE.
PERHAPS WE REALLY SHOULD HAVE WAITED
BEFORE YOU TOOK YOUR BROTHER'S THRONE!
  CLAUDIUS.
BUT NOW THAT HE HAS BEEN CREMATED—
  GERTRUDE/CLAUDIUS.
—WE OUGHT TO START A LITTLE FIRE OF OUR OWN!
  ALL.
SO START THE CELEBRATION!
FILL THE GOBLET, HEAP THE PLATE!
  GERTRUDE/CLAUDIUS.
ON OUR WEDDED JOURNEY LET OUR FEET MOVE
  FAST!
  ALL.
THE SKIES OF GRAY HAVE BLOWN AWAY!
A SUNNY DAY DRAWS NEAR!
  GERTRUDE.
WITH GEMS MY GOWN I'LL NOW BE ADORNING!
  CLAUDIUS.
NO MORE FROWNS OR MEM'RIES OF MOURNING!

ALL.
CALL THE CLOWNS AS JOY IS A-BORNING HERE!
GERTRUDE/CLAUDIUS.
AND SO, FAREWELL TO WOE!
ALL.
LET'S OVERFLOW WITH CHEER!

(*song's over; CLAUDIUS and GERTRUDE sit on thrones;
LIGHTING shifts to only the G-H-I area, where HAMLET
and HORATIO [still where we left them] now face downstage
again, for:*)

HAMLET. O! that this too too solid flesh would melt, thaw and resolve itself into a dew!

OPHELIA. (*enters via B, with a wistful smile*) Boy, I know *just* what you mean! (*links arms with HAMLET*) If I scarf one more hors d'oeuvre I'm gonna upchuck!

HORATIO. You *left* something, I hope — ?!

OPHELIA. Oh, sure! And they're refilling the buffet tables fast as we deplete 'em!

HORATIO. Terrific! Excuse me! (*bolts out via B*)

HAMLET. In thy garment of white, thou'rt ill-dressed for mourning, fair maid.

OPHELIA. Oh, the funeral was *hours* ago, Hammy! Lighten up! Do you have to go mooning all over the castle in that Johnny Cash costume?! [*NOTE: Or "Zorro costume"; suit yourself*]

HAMLET. Make you so light of my father's passage?

OPHELIA. Of course not, silly! But it's not as though he was a *spring chicken*, after all! We've *all* gotta go *some* time!

HAMLET. 'Tis not so much the suddenness of his departure as it is the precipitate gallop into wedlock of his widow that does rack my very heart! Would that I had eschewed *both* mournful ceremonies and remained away at college!

OPHELIA. Oh! That reminds me! I was trying to find you earlier to tell you that a pair of your old college buddies showed up at the drawbridge a few minutes ago!

HAMLET. Ah, then mayhap in *them* shall I find the sympathy I seek elsewhere in vain! Which two friends are these?

OPHELIA. One's called Rosie Krantz, the other one Gilda Stern. (*glances out through B*) Oh, say — there they come *now*!

[*NOTE: The upcoming "SEGUE" number has the* same *chore-*

ography each time it occurs in this show: Participants enter moving sideways, arms linked at the elbow, and do that "sidle-step" in which — starting with feet together — the right foot (if they're crossing from the right — otherwise all directions are reversed) moves across in front of the left, then the left foot is brought alongside the right, then the right foot moves across behind the left, and finally the left foot is brought alongside the right — this pattern repeats as often as necessary to effect a full cross of the stagefront from B to C (or vice-versa), and the number should be timed so that the final note sounds just as the crossers vanish. In other words, the participants enter (via B or C) on the first word of the number and exit on the last word of the number. Clear? Okay, then:]

ROSIE/GILDA. (*MUSIC INTROS and they cross/sing from B to C:*)
THOUGH WE'RE JUST OUT OF COLLEGE,
WE'RE SOMEWHAT SHORT ON KNOWLEDGE!
WE REALLY SHOULD APOLOG-
IZE FOR GOOFING OFF IN CLASS!
AS SCHOLARS WE'RE SUPREMELY
UNLEARN-ED AND UNSEEMLY!
AT LEAST WE'RE BOTH EXTREMELY
PRETTY IN OUR LOOKING-GLASS! (*they are gone*)

OPHELIA. Peppy little things, aren't they!

HAMLET. (*crossing toward C*) I must greet my great and good friends properly!

OPHELIA. I'll be at the buffet table if you need me! (*exits via B; ROSIE and GILDA re-enter via C just as HAMLET gets there*)

ROSIE. Hiii!

HAMLET. My sweet Rosie!

GILDA. This is a *groovy* castle you've got here!

HAMLET. Thank you, Gilda. *I've* always thought so — until today, at least! The cremation of my father the king has rather cast a chill upon my temper! I fear I am far too deeply engaged in mourning to be a truly gracious host.

ROSIE/GILDA. But aren't you glad to *see* us?

HAMLET. (*links arms with them*) Of *course* I am! (*and MUSIC INTROS, and he is just as perky as they, as all three now move from C-area toward B, during the song:*)
I FIND IT QUITE EXQUISITE
THAT YOU HAVE COME TO VISIT!

ALAS, I'M FAR TOO BUSY TO
ENJOY YOUR COMPANY!
  Rosie/Gilda.
WE'RE NOT THE LEAST BIT SLIGHTED!
WE'RE GLAD WE WERE INVITED!
WE'RE HAPPY AND DELIGHTED
TO HOBNOB WITH ROYALTY!

(*they are gone; LIGHTS COME UP FULL*)

Claudius. Saw you that? Meseems our glum young prince has found felicity in friendship!

Gertrude. I do hope so, my husband. For the sorrows of the earlier part of the day do weigh much too ponderously upon him!

Claudius. That reminds me — I guess we can get rid of *these* now — ! (*removes her mourning-band, and she removes his*)

Gertrude. Glad you thought of it! They'd look pretty silly in the *wedding*-pictures!

Claudius. Say, where *is* that photographer, anyhow?

Courtier. Sire, he did dawdle beside the buffet on his arrival.

Gertrude. Then let us hasten there apace and thus ensure our pictorial posterity!

Court. Huh?

Claudius. She means let's go get our picture took! (*links arms with GERTRUDE*) Come on, Queen!

(*ALL exit via A; the moment the last one has gone, HAMLET re-enters via B, his manner downcast*)

Hamlet. Mayhap I *do* cast a pall of gloom upon these festive proceedings. And yet — and yet — something within me says that all is not aright in these events. I know not wherefrom this suspicion springs — and yet — and yet —

(*GHOST enters via arras [NOTE: This curtain should be secured to the columns at its sides so it does not gap, but should be passed through easily at the central overlap of its two halves]; GHOST wears a battle helmet that hides its face, excepting the mouth*)

Ghost. Hamlet my son!

Hamlet. (*whirls to face sound of voice; reacts*) My father's ghost!

(*LIGHTS now only illuminate area including platform D and bench; HAMLET moves into area between bench and arras, during:*)

GHOST. Aye, the same!

HAMLET. And wherefore do you return from beyond this world to manifest thyself to me?

GHOST. I need a favor, Junior.

HAMLET. Thou've but to speak it and it shall I grant!

GHOST. Is that a yes or a no?

HAMLET. Name the favor and I'll do't!

GHOST. "Doot"?

HAMLET. (*enunciating carefully*) Do . . . it! Okay?

GHOST. Then be it known to thee that mine death was not an natural one!

HAMLET. O my prophetic soul! Then thy sudden passage was assisted?

GHOST. By the juice of curs-ed henbane in the portals of mine ear!

HAMLET. (*shocked*) In your ear!

GHOST. No, *really* . . . And awash with woe does my spirit seek thy saving succor e'en now!

HAMLET. Alas! (*MUSIC INTROS, and he sings:*)

OH, DAD!
YOU'RE LOOKING SO SAD
THAT I
AM WONDERING WHY!
YOUR ATTITUDE'S
SO SPOOKY THAT I FEEL CREEPY AND WEIRD!
MY GRATITUDE
YOU'D EARN IF YOU'D EXPLAIN WHY YOU'VE
    APPEARED!
I'VE HAD
A FEELING SO BAD
THAT MY
SUSPICIONS ARE HIGH
THAT YOUR DEMISE SO AGONIZING
SOMEHOW WASN'T RIGHT!
THERE'S SOMETHING ROTTEN IN DENMARK
    TONIGHT!
GHOST.
YOU'RE NOT KIDDING!
PUT THE BLAME ON MY BROTHER!

HE'S THE VILLAIN UNKNOWN!
LUSTING AFTER YOUR MOTHER
(NOT TO MENTION MY THRONE!),
LATE LAST WEEK HE CREPT UP WHERE I LAY
IN THE GARDEN WHERE I'D HIT THE HAY!
FROM HIS POCKET A PHIAL
FILLED WITH POISON, I FEAR,
SOON HAD EMPTIED ITS VILE
CONTENTS INTO MY EAR!
THE LAST THING I SAW WAS HIS TRIUMPHANT GRIN!
OH, BLAME YOUR UNCLE FOR DOING ME IN!
    HAMLET/GHOST.
(*overlapping*)
    I CAN'T BELIEVE IT!/PLEASE BELIEVE IT!
(*BOTH now repeat their parts in counterpoint, finishing:*)
    GHOST.
OH, BLAME YOUR UNCLE,
THAT MISBEGOTTEN MAN ON—
    HAMLET.
(*overlapping*)
THERE'S SOMETHING ROTTEN
AND MISBEGOTTEN UPON—
    BOTH.
—THE THRONE OF OUR LAND,
AND SWEET REVENGE NOW
IS SURELY AT HAND!
    GHOST.
SON, DO YOU UNDERSTAND?

(*song's over; HAMLET thrusts a forefinger skyward to vow:*)

    HAMLET. This day shall I wreak reciprocal ravagement upon that miscreant poltroon!
    GHOST. Is that a yes or a no?
    HAMLET. Verily, 'tis yea!
    GHOST. Oh, good. (*starts to exit*)
    HAMLET. (*slyly*) But first shall I contrive to convince one and all that I have gone mad!
    GHOST. (*pauses at flap of arras*) What in the world *for*?
    HAMLET. To make easier my avengement upon thy slayer!
    GHOST. But how will acting *nutty* help?
    HAMLET. Well, see, once I start acting goofy, everybody will

think—that is, Claudius will think—or rather, the word will get out that—um— Come to think of it, I don't have the slightest idea! But it's the only plan I've got!

GHOST. Lotsa luck, fella!

(*exits via arras* [*NOTE: If lighting is such that the GHOST cannot go behind the arras and (right now) depart from behind the arras without the audience noticing him during the moments that area is in darkness, then you'd better have an "escape" in the upstage wall there for him*]).

HAMLET. (*moves down into G area and LIGHTING now illuminates G-H-I area only*) Now shall I counterfeit the countenance of craziness and trepidatiously trigger my trap! (*gives wild laugh and exits via B; a moment later we hear:*)

POLONIUS. (*offstage near C*) Furthermore, my son Laertes, before you do return to your university studies, a few more fatherly advices would I give thee . . . [*NOTE: If you are* not *"doubling" LAERTES in the GHOST role, have the twosome enter* immediately *at start of foregoing speech; otherwise, have POLONIUS delay his entrance until LAERTES can appear "as himself," suitcase in hand, trailing politely but wearily after his father as they cross from C to exit via B; their speeches should be timed so that they cross and exit at an unbroken pace, vanishing via B fractionally before the last few syllables are spoken.*] Beware of entrance to a quarrel, but, being in, bear it that the opposed may beware of thee.

LAERTES. (*perfunctorily, not really paying attention*) Yes, Dad.

POLONIUS. Give every man thy ear, but few thy voice; take each man's censure, but reserve thy judgment.

LAERTES. Yes, Dad.

POLONIUS. Costly thy habit as thy purse can buy, but not expressed in fancy; rich, not gaudy; for the apparel oft proclaims the man.

(*if you haven't guessed, POLONIUS moves in old-mannish short shuffling steps, so that he has plenty of time to Babble All before they exit*)

LAERTES. Whatever you say, Dad.

POLONIUS. Neither a borrower, nor a lender be; for loan oft

loses both itself and friend, and borrowing dulls the edge of husbandry.

LAERTES. Wouldn't want *that* to happen.

POLONIUS. This above all: To thine own self be true, and it must follow, as the night the day, thou canst not then — (*he exits via B during:*) —be false to any man . . .

LAERTES. (*exits after him on:*) Yeah-yeah, sure-sure, whatever!

(*LIGHTS COME UP FULL and immediately HORATIO enters via A, toting a trayful of food, followed on by OPHE-LIA; BOTH move down toward C during:*)

HORATIO. Never *saw* so many people gorging at one time! There *must* be a chair *someplace!* (*hesitates before thrones; eyes them speculatively*)

OPHELIA. Don't you *dare!* That photography session won't last *forever!*

HORATIO. You're right; bad idea. (*continues onward toward C, during:*)

OPHELIA. I wonder where the prince has got to. Talk about your party-poopers!

HORATIO. He *is* being kind of a glump today. Probably something he ate. I'm going to try for one of those tables out in the garden. (*exits via C*)

OPHELIA. Save me a place. I'll give one more look around for Hammy, and if I can't find him, I'll get a plate and join you!

HORATIO. (*off*) Bring some of that *rumaki*, will you? I didn't have room on my tray!

(*OPHELIA nods, turns, and starts toward B, but stops as HAM-LET enters via B; his hair is mussed, his tunic partially unbuttoned, and he wears a garland of daisies about his neck; he sees her, comes to a stop*)

OPHELIA. (*studies him for a second; then:*) Oh, *good*, you've cheered up!

HAMLET. Nay-nay. These are the trappings of madness!

OPHELIA. What are you *mad* about?

HAMLET. In my weakened mental state, I have decided forever to forswear thy love!

OPHELIA. Oh, come off it! You've just got premarital jitters. *All* fiances feel like that. Now how about a kiss!

HAMLET. It were wise that thee *also* remove thyself from romance! Earthly passions are but the matter of a moment!

OPHELIA. But *what* a moment! (*tries to embrace him; he holds her off with one extended arm*)

HAMLET. Not for *us* the fleeting foolishness of transitory treasures! Now give me back that promissory ring I did bestow upon thee!

OPHELIA. (*looks at ring on her finger*) Rich gifts wax poor when givers prove unkind . . . (*pulls back as he tries to take ring*) But *this* rock is nearly *two carats*, kiddo! Besides, I don't *want* to break off our engagement!

HAMLET. Sorrow not, sweet maiden! Our love can nevermore be! In Denmark, it's illegal to marry a certifiable nutcake!

OPHELIA. (*angry, fists on hips, flashes:*) *Who* you calling a nutcake?!

HAMLET. Not *you*, Ophy—I mean *me*! Now, let us part as good friends—thou to thy chamber, me to my madness!

OPHELIA. You don't dump me *that* easily, Ham! I'm gonna call my lawyer!

HAMLET. (*grabs her before she can go*) But I *am* gone mad! You've got to believe me—and you've got to be brave about it! (*MUSIC INTROS, and he sings:*)
PRITHEE, BABY, STAND FAST
THOUGH THIS DAY BE OUR LAST!
LOVE'S JUST NOT WORTH THE TROUBLE!
FLEE ITS UNEARTHLY GRIP
AND RUN OFF ON THE DOUBLE!

PRITHEE, BABY, I'M THROUGH
WITH THEE, BABY, IT'S TRUE!
SOME FOLKS SAY WE
SHOULD MAKING HAY BE,
BUT PRITHEE, BABY,
ADIEU!
(*releases her, starts to go, but now* she *grabs* him)
OPHELIA.
WHAT HAVE I DONE, LORD HAMLET?
YOUR MANNER IS QUITE FORBIDDING!
YOU SAY YOU DON'T GIVE A DAMN, YET
MY HEART INSISTS YOU'RE ONLY KIDDING!
(*tries to snuggle up cozily against him, but he pulls free, and now he will dodge here and there about the stage, trying to evade her grasp, as she continues cheerily:*)

PRITHEE, BABY, YOU'RE WRONG!
Hamlet.
BUT LOVE IS PURE BALONEY!
Ophelia.
WE'LL MAKE HAY BEFORE LONG!
Hamlet.
STOP TALKING MATRIMONY!
I PREFER THEE STAY SINGLE!
Ophelia.
BUT MISSES DON'T GET KISSES!
Hamlet.
I'M UNWORTHY
TO MAKE THY MAIDEN'S PULSES TINGLE!
Ophelia.
PRITHEE, BABY, BE NICE!
Hamlet.
ALL TIES I PLAN TO SEVER!
Ophelia.
LOVE ALONE WILL SUFFICE!
Hamlet.
WE'VE HIT THE FAN FOREVER!
Ophelia. (*shoves him down onto bench*)
LET'S GO APEY!
Hamlet.
I DON'T MEAN MAYBE!
Ophelia. (*sits on his lap*)
OH, PRITHEE, BABY!

Hamlet.
NO DICE!
(*she embraces him; he squirms to free himself during:*)
PRITHEE, BABY, RELAX!
Ophelia.
YOU DO ROMANCE DISSERVICE!
Hamlet.
ROMANCE JUST GOT THE AX!
Ophelia.
YOUR SQUIRMING MAKES ME NERVOUS!
BE A CHUM, DO!
Hamlet. (*gives up, embraces her glumly*)
OH, WHERE'S A THUMBSCREW?!
Both. (*cheek-to-cheek out front:*)
THIS SETUP'S DUMB TO THE MAX!

(*MUSIC STOPS; they kiss, briefly, then he manages to get her off his lap and stand up, and back away slowly toward C*)

HAMLET. Farewell, sweet maiden!

(*extends his arms toward her, moaning and sighing, but continues backward until he exits via C; nonplussed, she sits on bench, staring uncertainly after him; then POLONIUS enters via B*)

OPHELIA. Father! When was the last time Prince Hamlet went in for a checkup? He's acting so *nutty*— moaning, sighing, clothing all unbuttoned. Unless maybe he's been hitting the schnapps—?

POLONIUS. Alas, 'tis as I feared! His grief for his father has robbed him of his wits! I must hurry hence and tell his mother! (*GERTRUDE and CLAUDIUS enter via A at this moment, headed throneward*)

OPHELIA. No need! Here she is now! Excuse me, I've gotta go find a fruitcake! (*exits, fast, via C*)

POLONIUS. (*shuffling excitedly up toward thrones, arriving there just as GERTRUDE and CLAUDIUS sit down*) Alas, alas, I do dreadful tidings bring!

CLAUDIUS. Ah, but what dire news cannot my royal majesty make aright with a proclamation?

POLONIUS. I do fear this misfortune lies beyond the powers of majesty!

GERTRUDE. Laertes missed his boat?

POLONIUS. Worse, Madam: Prince Hamlet has lost his wits!

GERTRUDE. What are you saying, Polonius?

POLONIUS. We must ascertain a reason for the passing of reason — find out the cause of this effect, or rather say, the cause of this defect, for this effect defective comes by cause!

CLAUDIUS. Huh?

GERTRUDE. (*to POLONIUS, patiently*) More matter, with less art.

CLAUDIUS. Are you telling us Prince Hamlet is mad?

POLONIUS. That he is mad, 'tis true; 'tis true 'tis pity; and pity 'tis 'tis true!

CLAUDIUS. (*to GERTRUDE*) Does that mean what I think it means?

GERTRUDE. *Whatever* it means, get ready for a long session — Polonius, to be brief, has never *managed* to be brief!

CLAUDIUS. Now he's got *you* doing it! . . . Polonius, if what you say is so, then this matter must not be made privy to all and sundry; rather should we somehow contrive to conceal the affliction by royal restriction and brand it a fiction!

GERTRUDE. Now he's got *you* doing it! . . . Polonius, we *must* keep matters mum!

CLAUDIUS. But for how long can the secret be kept? Polonius, do you have any suggestion what our course should be?

(*MUSIC INTROS, and:*)

POLONIUS. (*sings*)
WHAT TO DO?! WHAT TO DO?!
I HAVE NOT A SINGLE CLUE!
GERTRUDE.
IF IT'S TRUE, LET'S REVIEW—
ALL.
—HOW WE BEST CAN KEEP IT SECRET!
CLAUDIUS.
OFF HIS BLOCK! SUCH A SHOCK!
WE WILL BE A LAUGHINGSTOCK!
GERTRUDE.
LUNACY SURE CAN BE—
ALL.
—ROUGH ON ROYALTY!
CLAUDIUS.
THOUGH WE ARE AGHAST,
AND WE DEPLORE IT—
GERTRUDE.
—RUMOR DOESN'T LAST
ETERNALLY!
POLONIUS.
TIME'S A REMEDY!
GERTRUDE.
BUT HOW LONG MUST WE—
ALL.
—IGNORE IT
BEFORE IT
FADES IN THE MIST
OF HISTORY?
CLAUDIUS.
IT'S A PAIN!

GERTRUDE.
BUT IT'S PLAIN
THAT—
    ALL.
—IF THE PRINCE IS NOT QUITE SANE—
    POLONIUS.
—KEEP IT MUM!
    GERTRUDE.
JUST PLAY DUMB!
    ALL.
SAY HE'S RIGHT AS RAIN!
    GERTRUDE.
SO, HERE'S OUR PLAN:
    CLAUDIUS.
LET'S BE STILL!
    ALL.
THOUGH HE'S AN
IMBECILE,
WE'LL GIVE OUT NO IFS OR ANDS OR BUTS!
NO HINTS
THE ROYAL PRINCE
IS NUTS!

(*upstage area goes dark as LIGHTING now only illuminates
    area G-H-I; CLAUDIUS, GERTRUDE and POLONIUS
    will exit via A as MUSIC INTROS, and:*)

ROSIE/GILDA. (*doing sing/cross from C to B:*)
POOR HAMLET'S SUCH A DUMMY!
THE SITUATION'S CRUMMY!
JUST HOW CAN WE BE CHUMMY
WHEN A LUCID MIND HE AIN'T?
WE CAN'T BE POLLYANNAS
NOW THAT HE'S GONE BANANAS!
SO CHAFE OUR WRISTS AND FAN US
'CAUSE WE'RE FEELING RATHER FAINT!

(*they are gone, via B; a moment later, HAMLET enters via C, his
    hair combed, daisies gone, and shirt buttoned; he moves to
    area H, faces solemnly out front, MUSIC INTROS, AND:*)

HAMLET. (*sings solemnly:*)
TO BE . . .

(*FULL LIGHTS UP instantly, as TROUPERS peek [heads only] onstage at archways A, B and C, and:*)

TROUPERS.
TO BE!
(*they duck from sight instantly as HAMLET turns, sees no one, shrugs away his puzzlement, and continues:*)

HAMLET.
OR NOT . . .
  TROUPERS. (*same business*)
   . . . *TO BE!*
(*this time HAMLET manages to spot them before they duck away; he looks out at us, smiles shrewdly, and then:*)
  HAMLET. (*with lightning speed:*)
THAT-IS-THE-QUESTION!
(*declares to just-popping-in TROUPERS:*)
GOTCHA!
(*they slump, caught, and remain in view as he continues, doing a kind of light-softshoe:*)
WHETH- . . . ER . . . 'TIS . . .
NOBLER IN THE MIND TO SUFFER . . .
  TROUPERS. (*softshoeing onstage similarly*)
 . . . THE SLINGS AND ARROWS OF OUTRAGEOUS FORTUNE . . .
  HAMLET. (*as TROUPERS dance into line-formation upstage of him*)
 . . . OR TO TAKE ARMS AGAINST A SEA OF TROUBLES, AND BY OPPOSING END THEM?
  TROUPERS.
OR AT LEAST BEND THEM!
(*MUSIC suddenly becomes red-hot samba, ALL dancing on:*)
  HAMLET.
TO DIE . . .
  TROUPERS.
TO SLEEP . . .
  HAMLET.
NO MORE . . .

ALL.
AND BY A SLEEP TO SAY WE END THE
  HEARTACHE . . .
TROUPERS.
AND THE THOUSAND NATURAL SHOCKS THAT
FLESH IS HEIR TO—
HAMLET.
—WHEN WE DARE TO—
ALL.
'TIS A CONSUMMATION
DEVOUTLY TO BE WISHED.
HAMLET.
TO DIE . . .
TROUPERS.
TO SLEEP . . .
HAMLET.
TO SLEEP . . .
TROUPERS.
PERCHANCE TO *DREAM*! (*this last syllable on an
  ominous chord; samba is over, now, as:*)
HAMLET.
(*declaims*)
AY, THERE'S THE RUB:
(*sings again:*)
FOR . . . (*next segment is sung super-fast in "patter-song"
  tempo*)
ALL.
. . . IN THAT SLEEP OF DEATH WHAT DREAMS
MAY COME, WHEN WE HAVE SHUFFLED OFF THIS
MORTAL COIL,
MUST GIVE US PAUSE!
(*All pause; then Hamlet takes a step further down front,
  like a friendly orator addressing his audience, while
  TROUPERS quietly gather into bass-baritone-tenor-
  whatever groupings upstage of him for:*)
HAMLET.
(*declaiming*) THERE'S THE RESPECT THAT MAKES
  CALAMITY OF SO LONG LIFE!
TROUPERS.
(*waving "bye-bye" toward audience, sing:*) SO LONG, LIFE!
HAMLET.
FOR WHO WOULD BEAR THE WHIPS AND SCORNS
  OF TIME . . .

TROUPERS.
(*solemnly*) DOO-WAH!
  HAMLET.
THE OPPRESSOR'S WRONG . . .
  TROUPERS.
DOO-WAH!
  HAMLET.
THE PROUD MAN'S CONTUMELY . . .
  TROUPERS.
DOO-WAH!
  HAMLET.
THE PANGS OF DISPRIZED LOVE . . .
  TROUPERS.
DOO-WAH!
  HAMLET.
THE LAW'S DELAY . . .
  TROUPERS.
DOO-WAH!
  HAMLET.
THE INSOLENCE OF OFFICE . . .
  TROUPERS.
DOO-WAH!
  HAMLET.
AND THE SPURNS THAT PATIENT MERIT OF THE
  UNWORTHY TAKES—!
  TROUPERS.
(look *as if they're about to "Doo-wah!" again, but then
they do a "double take," jam fists to hips, and query:*)
WHAT THE HELL DOES *THAT* MEAN?
  HAMLET.
(*shrugs, smiles guiltily*) SEARCH *ME*! *I'M* STILL
WORKING ON *"CONTUMELY"*! (*they chuckle, and
he continues:*) . . . WHEN HE HIMSELF MIGHT HIS
QUIETUS MAKE WITH A BARE BODKIN?
  TROUPERS.
(*each with a hand-to-stomach grimace of pain*) OOH! AH!
  HAMLET.
WHO WOULD FARDELS BEAR—
  TROUPERS.
(*sing perkily*) OLD MAN FARDEL HAD A BEAR!
  (*HAMLET gives them an icy glare; they look abashed
  and fall silent; then, dignity restored, he faces us once
  again, and:*)

HAMLET.
... TO GRUNT AND SWEAT UNDER A WEARY
LIFE ... (*will start singing again*)
BUT ... THAT ...
ALL. (*softshoe again*)
THE ...
DREAD OF SOMETHING AFTER
DEATH, THE UNDISCOVERED COUNTRY ...
HAMLET.
FROM WHOSE BOURN NO TRAVELER RETURNS ...
TROUPERS.
PUZZLES THE WILL ...
HAMLET.
AND MAKES US RATHER BEAR
THOSE ILLS WE HAVE—
TROUPERS.
LA-LA-LA-LA!
HAMLET.
—THAN FLY TO OTHERS THAT WE KNOW NOT
OF? (*he will join TROUPER's line, at center, as:*)
ALL (*dancing as they sing:*)
THUS CONSCIENCE DOTH MAKE COWARDS OF US
ALL!
NO MATTER IF YOUR BACK IS TO THE WALL,
YOU'D RATHER FACE THE AXE THAT'S DUE TO FALL
THAN INITIATE THE DOOM BY YOURSELF! (*ALL
start high-kicking strut-exit toward B*)
SO PUT THAT BIG, BAD BODKIN
BACK ON THE SHELF! (*will cakewalk-strut exit via B, during:*)
PUT IT BACK ON THE SHELF ... ! (*they are gone*)

(*the moment they are off, POLONIUS enters via A with CLAU-
DIUS, moving toward arras, he eager, CLAUDIUS
reluctant*)
POLONIUS. Come, sire, let us hide behind the arras!
CLAUDIUS. *Olivia de Havilland?!*
POLONIUS. *This* arras! Now here is my plan, sire. I have com-
pelled my daughter, who virtuously obeys me in all things, to
arrange a meeting down there by yon bench with young Prince
Hamlet, that in our overhearing their converse whilst secreted
from their view here behind this arras, we may ascertain the depth
of his depravity! (*BOTH have halted in* front *of arras now*)

CLAUDIUS. I like it not! To eavesdrop is beneath the dignity of a king!

POLONIUS. Then do but keep me company, sire, while *I* do so! (*enters through overlap into area behind arras*)

CLAUDIUS. Oh, well, if you put it like *that* . . . (*exits behind arras after him; the moment they are concealed, OPHELIA enters via C, looks about, moves timidly to area just below bench*)

OPHELIA. Hamlet? Lord Hamlet? Yoo-hoo! Hammy?

HAMLET. (*enters via B; he is once again hair-rumpled, unbuttoned and daisied*) Who calls my name? Why, what sweet creature is this?

OPHELIA. Oh, stop acting so nutty! You know darn well! Now, let's settle this once and for all: Are we still engaged, or aren't we?! (*upstage, POLONIUS furtively peeks around from behind left column, simultaneous with CLAUDIUS peeking around from behind right column, during:*)

HAMLET. (*hesitates, then after a quick peek toward B and C, moves a bit closer to her and speaks in lowered, confidential tones*) As to that, fair maiden, there is a truth I feel conjoined to impart to thee. You see, in actuality I am not—

(*notices that she's staring at something behind him; he turns his head swiftly, and just as swiftly CLAUDIUS and PO-LONIUS duck from view; but he has seen them, and when he faces OPHELIA again, his eyes are shrewd*)

OPHELIA. Continue please, my lord—? In actuality, you are not—?

HAMLET. (*in tones of mad bravado*) I am not fit to sully thy flesh by my touch! Nor is any man! Thou'rt far too fair to be the object of earthly desires! Men are not *suited* to marriage! Have you *none* of them! (*MUSIC INTROS, and he sings:*)
A MAN IS A CRUEL CREATURE!

OPHELIA.
BUT MEN ARE SO COOL!

HAMLET.
THE HEART IS A FOOLISH TEACHER!

OPHELIA.
LOVE ISN'T A SCHOOL!

HAMLET.
THE WORLD IS HORRID AND VILE!

OPHELIA.
DON'T BE A DROOP,
YOU PARTY-POOP!
    HAMLET.
A CLOISTER'S MORE IN YOUR STYLE!
    OPHELIA.
TO BE A NUN
FOR ME'S NO FUN!
    POLONIUS. (*in view again, singing to CLAUDIUS, also in view again*)
HE CERTAINLY SOUNDS CLEARHEADED!
    CLAUDIUS.
HIS MANNER'S NOT MAD!
    POLONIUS.
IT MAY BE LESS THAN WE DREADED!
(*comes from behind pillar, as does CLAUDIUS*)
    CLAUDIUS.
I THINK I'VE BEEN HAD!
    OPHELIA.
I PREFER TO MARRY
AND START A FAMILY!
    HAMLET.
NO, GET THEE TO A NUNNERY!
(*via A, B and C, TROUPERS and ELSINORITAS enter, in couples, walking in tempo as they chant:*)
    CHORUS.
GET THEE TO A NUNNERY! GET THEE TO A NUNNERY!
GET THEE TO A NUNNERY! GET THEE TO A NUNNERY!
(*abruptly, a wild* Charleston *begins, and ALL dance to it, during:*)
    POLONIUS. (*for this number, dances perkily as a youth*)
DANCING THUS IS RATHER PRECARIOUS!
    CLAUDIUS.
BUT YOU MUST ADMIT IT'S GREGARIOUS!
    CHORUS.
LET'S BE JUST: IT'S REALLY HILARIOUS
TRYING TO STAY ON YOUR FEET!
    HAMLET.
MUSIC'S SOMEHOW SHAKIN' THE BLUES AWAY!
    OPHELIA.
TROUBLES MELT AND SUDDENLY OOZE AWAY!

CHORUS.
YOU CAN'T MOPE WHILE DANCIN' YOUR SHOES
    AWAY
TO A BLITHE AND BEAUTIFUL BEAT!
(*ALL are in G-H-I area, now, happy as a clam*)
    HAMLET.
IT'S RATHER HARD
TO REMAIN DESPONDENT!
    OPHELIA.
LET'S DISREGARD
THAT OLD DANISH CONVENT!
    CLAUDIUS.
HEAR THE BAND!
    POLONIUS.
HOLD HER HAND!
    CHORUS.
DON'T BE SUCH A WITHDRAWN GENT!
(*though* Charleston *ends here, ALL continue to move
    rhythmically in modified dancing during:*)
    OPHELIA.
YOU'RE TRULY A DARLING DANCER!
    HAMLET.
LET GO OF MY ARM!
    CLAUDIUS.
HIS ATTITUDE WON'T ENTRANCE HER!
    POLONIUS.
HE MEANS HER NO HARM!
    HAMLET. (*trying to revert to, and remain evincing,
heartlessness*)
THE CONVENT'S WHERE YOU BELONG!
    OPHELIA.
I'M MUCH TOO GAY
TO LOCK AWAY!
    CLAUDIUS.
IF THIS IS LOVE, IT'S ALL WRONG!
    POLONIUS.
HE'S SUCH A CLOD! IT'S VERY ODD!
    CHORUS.
YOU REALLY CANNOT DISMISS HER!
    OPHELIA.
I PINE TO BE HIS!
    CHORUS.
YOU OUGHTA GIVE IN AND KISS HER!

HAMLET.
OH, MIND YOUR OWN BIZ!
OPHELIA.
BEING A RELIGIOUS
DOES NOT APPEAL TO ME!
HAMLET.
A NUNNERY IS WHERE YOU SHOULD BE!
OPHELIA. (*shoves him down onto bench*)
MY LOVE'S SO PRODIGIOUS!
HAMLET. (*as she sits on his lap*)
STOP CLIMBING ON MY KNEE!
OPHELIA.
IT'S FUN—
HAMLET.
IT'S VANITY!
OPHELIA.
TO—
HAMLET.
INSANITY!
OPHELIA.
SHUN—
CLAUDIUS.
HE'S GRINNING NOW!
(*and HAMLET is, too, finally embracing OPHELIA back*)
OPHELIA.
A—
POLONIUS.
SHE'S WINNING NOW!
HAMLET/OPHELIA.
NUN-
OTHERS.
IT'S EVIDENT—
HAMLET/OPHELIA.
—NER—
OTHERS.
—THOSE TWO WERE MEANT—
HAMLET/OPHELIA.
—Y!
OTHERS.
—FOR MATRIMONY!
ALL. (*shout*)
WHEE!

*(at song's end, excepting HAMLET and OPHELIA, ALL
    OTHERS exit in various groups, chuckling merrily and very
    much in a party mood; after a moment:)*

HAMLET. (*quietly*) You can get off my lap now.

OPHELIA. Sorry, milord. I got carried away. (*will slip from his
lap to set on bench beside him*)

HAMLET. I don't think for one *minute* Claudius believes I'm
off my rocker!

OPHELIA. Why *should* he? You're *not* off your rocker!

HAMLET. But I want everyone to *think* I am!

OPHELIA. What in the world *for*?!

HAMLET. (*shrugs*) It's the only plan I've *got*! Somehow, I
thought it might help me to kill my uncle — I'm not *sure* exactly
how it's supposed to help.

OPHELIA. Kill your uncle?! Why would you want to kill your
uncle?!

HAMLET. For murdering my father!

OPHELIA. Murdering your—?! Oh, come *on*, now, Hammy!
Where did you get a silly idea like that?

HAMLET. (*solemnly*) From my father's ghost!

OPHELIA. Hey, maybe you *are* a little looney!

HAMLET. I tell you, my father's ghost appeared to me and said
Claudius killed him!

OPHELIA. But why have *you* avenge him? Why doesn't he just
appear to *Claudius* and *scare* him to death?!

HAMLET. Gee, why didn't *I* think of that?!

OPHELIA. Look, Hammy, it seems to me that *you* ought to do a
little more *checking* before you go around killing kings. What if
you only *imagined* you saw a ghost?

HAMLET. Impossible! I mean — it was so *real* . . .

OPHELIA. So's a *nightmare* till you wake *up* from it!

HAMLET. I wonder if perhaps I *am* a bit mentally disturbed?

OPHELIA. The *nut* is always the last to know! And how about
this: Let's say you *did* see some kind of spirit — how do you know
it *was* your father? What if it's the *devil* trying to make you bump
off an innocent man?!

HAMLET. *Now* I *am* worried! What am I to do? If truly 'twas my
father, I should follow out my plan of revenge — but if it were an
evil spirit, I should forswear such an undertaking! What do *you*
suggest?

OPHELIA. Well, let's consider the facts . . .

(MUSIC INTROS and they sing:)

HAMLET/OPHELIA.
MAYBE 'TWAS A DEVIL
WITH LIES FROM HELL!
BUT IF IT'S ON THE LEVEL
THEN ALL'S NOT WELL!
IS THERE NOT SOME TEST
OF SIGNIFICANCE
THAT WOULD MANIFEST
GUILT OR INNOCENCE?
WHAT WE'VE GOT TO DO IS AIM
OUR EFFORTS TO PROVE
HE'S NOT BEREFT OF BLAME!
LET US STRETCH OUR RE-
SOURCES TO THE FULL!
IF IT'S TREACHERY,
WHERE'S THE CURE?
IN MATTERS SO ACUTE,
ONE MUST BE ABSOLUTELY SURE!
LEST WE BE PREMATURE,
IT'S PRUDENT TO BE SURE . . . !

(song's over; HAMLET stands up)

HAMLET. Well, if you think of anything, let me know.

OPHELIA. *(stands, takes his hands)* You can count on it. *(the BOTH look off via C as we hear the sound of revelry)*

HAMLET. Hark, I do hear the sound of revelry!

OPHELIA. It is that troupe of players your uncle has invited here for the wedding celebration.

HAMLET. From their hearty laughter, I rejoice they did *not* make it in time for the *funeral!*

(and then MUSIC INTROS, and they BOTH step back toward bench to be out of the way as a wildly motley group enters via C—some cartwheeling, some juggling, some sommersault-ing, etc.—it is our trusty CHORUS, or course, having re-cos-tumed into garish vaudevillian outfits [males and females, please, even though Shakespeare's era eschewed the latter in theatrical matters]; they will surround [but not block from view] HAMLET and OPHELIA, and sing and dance and cavort like crazy during:)

CHORUS.
BATTEN DOWN THE HATCHES!
HURRY HERE TO CATCH US!
WE'LL INCITE SHEER DELIGHT
LIKE A HURRICANE MEANT
FOR YOUR ENTERTAINMENT!
COME AND JUST WATCH OUR DUST!

HERE SHORTLY WILL EMERGE E-
RUPTIONS OF DRAMATURGY!
SO IF YOU FEEL THE URGE E-
NOUGH, WE WILL STRUT OUR
STUFF WITH A FLUTTER!

WANNA HEAR THE BAND? STAND
OVER BY THE GRANDSTAND!
OOM-PAH-PAH! OO-LA-LA!
BUT IF YOU ARE AFTER
UNABATED LAUGHTER
WE CAN DRAW YOUR GUFFAW!

CAST OFF YOUR DARK ENCHAINMENT
AND THAT MOOD OF BLUE,
'CAUSE WE ARE BRINGING ENTERTAINMENT
TO YOU!

(*HAMLET has been looking brighter by the moment, and now he
clutches OPHELIA excitedly by the upper arms, suddenly
inspired, as he and she BOTH enter into the song* [*CHORUS
listening eagerly to them*] *on:*)

HAMLET.
SUDDENLY A PLAN I'M HATCHING!
SUCH A VERY SIMPLE THING!
IN A PLAY I COULD BE CATCHING
THE CONSCIENCE OF THE KING!
    OPHELIA. (*dancing around him in delight*)
OH, WHAT A GOOD IDEA!
YOU COULD OVERSEE A
DRAMA WHICH MAKES HIM TWITCH!
    HAMLET. (*beckoning CHORUS nearer to huddle with him as
he explains:*)

T'LL BE TERRIFIC
PUTTING IN SPECIFIC
THINGS HE HAD DONE TO DAD!
WHERE'S A PAD AND PENCIL?!
LET US NOW COMMENCE A LITTLE ENDEAVOR!
  OPHELIA.
AND IF YOUR LIBRETTO
GETS HIM IN THE NET, OH, HAMLET, YOU'RE CLEVER!
  CHORUS. (*now mostly facing out front, while lifting HAMLET
and OPHELIA up to* stand *on the bench for maximal visibility to
us* [*after all, this* is *the first-act Finale, and they are principals*])
MERRY WE WILL MAKE
WHEN THERE IS NO MISTAKE
HIS CONSCIENCE IS AWAKENING!
  ALL. (*in high exaltation and excitement*)
FOR CATCHING THE KING
OUR LITTLE PLAY'S THE THING!
THE . . . PLAY'S . . . THE . . . THING . . . !

CURTAIN

End of ACT ONE

ACT TWO

At curtain-rise we find HAMLET trailing back and forth behind our trio from the CHORUS garbed as "Gertrude," "Claudius," and "King Hamlet"; each respectively has a large "G" and "C" and "H" on the chest of their costume; they are pacing and diligently studying scripts, paying little if any attention to our prince.

HAMLET. Speak the speech, I pray you, as I pronounced it to you, trippingly on the tongue; but if you mouth it, as many of your players do, I had as lief the town crier spoke my lines. (*OPHELIA enters via C, stops, listens, shakes her head in exasperation, and starts toward HAMLET'S back [she'll interrupt him just above bench]*) Nor do not saw the air too much with your hand, thus; but use all gently; for in the very torrent, tempest, and as I may say the whirlwind of passion, you must acquire and beget a temperance that —

OPHELIA. You know, Hammy, in a lot of ways you're quite like my *father*! Don't you ever run out of breath?! (*arm-tugs him down to the G-area during:*) Now leave these people alone! They have *lines* to learn!

HAMLET. But I was only trying to —

OPHELIA. Look, it's tough *enough* you having them do that old chestnut *The Murder of Gonzago* in the *first* place, without giving them all those extra lines and bits of business, besides! They'll be fine, just fine! Come on, let's share a cup of claret! (*almost tugs him off via B, but they stop as DIRECTOR and CHOREOGRAPHER [more stalwarts of the CHORUS] enter via C on:*)

DIRECTOR. *Places*, everybody! Showtime in five minutes! (*TRIO will hurry up to arras, duck through flap from our view*)

HAMLET. (*moving back toward I-area, OPHELIA trailing after him*) A thousand thanks to you, good director, for indulging my whim today! I had feared you would take umbrage at mine attempt to rework an established play.

DIRECTOR. No trouble at all. Oh, of course, we had to *fiddle* with your lines a *little* to make them *rhyme*.

HAMLET. Rhyme? Whatever *for*?

DIRECTOR. To fit the *tune*, of course! Didn't I tell you? My troupe does only *musicals*.

HAMLET. (*horrified*) You mean — when they do *The Murder of Gonzago* — they're going to *sing* it?!

34

OPHELIA. Let's hope they stay on *key*—or the king might vince for the wrong reasons!

DIRECTOR. Now-now, their voices are just fine. *And* their movements are—well—as perfect as achievable under the circumstances.

HAMLET. (*with foreboding*) *What* "circumstances" . . . ?

DIRECTOR. (*indicates companion*) Our choreographer is rather *new* at this line of work! He used to be a Bavarian *clockmaker!*

CHOREOGRAPHER. (*with heavy Germanic accent*) Bot eef I could make dose leetle teensy peoples on a *clock* to dance, vhy not *real* peoples, I asked mineself!

OPHELIA. (*uneasily*) And what did you *answer*?

HAMLET. This is madness! I planned a dark, turgid drama of foulest murder, and now you tell me it's going to be done in song-and-dance?!

CHOREOGRAPHER. (*proudly*) I got der showbiz in *mein blut!* *Sehr gut, ja*?

HAMLET. (*turns despondently to OPHELIA*) *Ach, Du Lieber!* then ALL react as we hear from offstage:)

MAJOR-DOMO. (*off*) Make way for his majesty the king—!

ACCOMPANIST will now play FANFARONADE as CLAU-
DIUS, GERTRUDE and COURT enter; the gimmick is this:
entering at A, it takes king and queen but three or four steps to
arrive at — and stand before — their thrones; the music, how-
ever, continues for at least twice *that length of time, building*
and building into a giddily soaring burst of regalness, pausing
only at CLAUDIUS's upcoming shout; got that? Okay, then,
FANFARONADE starts, MAJOR-DOMO enters via A, first,
announcing over the music:)

MAJOR-DOMO. His majesty the king!

GERTRUDE and CLAUDIUS arrive at thrones, stand waiting;
then:)

CLAUDIUS. (*as music reaches its peak*) All *right*, already! I'm here, I'm *here*!

then he and GERTRUDE both wince as ACCOMPANIST
quickly finishes the number with a totally unsuitable quick

jazz-wrapup; now the number is over; king and queen sit, and
HAMLET and OPHELIA will make their ways to sit on the
edge of the platform [E] downstage of thrones, and everyone in
view onstage generally fanning out to focus on the bench-area
[where the little show will take place], leaving clear the area
between arras and bench [NOTE: Our Gonzago trio will play
out front, to us, of course; if anyone else onstage notices
they're seeing only the "rear view" of the playlet, they cer-
tainly don't let on]; when all spectators are in place:)

CLAUDIUS. Let the play begin!

(LIGHTS will dim down to illuminate only the combined arras,
bench areas; the next line is said just before the dim-down is
complete)

HAMLET. (*to OPHELIA*) Now, keep an eye on the king, and
let's see how he reacts!

(only the playlet-areas can now be seen; MUSIC INTROS, and
it's such a ticky-tocky tempo we know we're in for trouble—
and then our dread is proven as "GERTRUDE" and "KING
HAMLET" enter via arras: They move [as will "CLAU-
DIUS" when he appears] exactly like mechanical clock-
figures—arms move with unbending elbows, legs with rigid
knees, heads wag side-to-side, etc. They'd make Pinocchio
look like Baryshnikov)

"HAMLET". (*sings*)
BEING KING'S VERY HARD.
   "GERTRUDE".
SEND AWAY THE GUARD,
AND RELAX HERE IN YOUR GARDEN!
YOU MAY LOSE ALL YOUR BLUES!
   "HAMLET".
I COULD USE A SNOOZE,
OR MY ARTERIES MIGHT HARDEN!
(*they will move to forefront of bench, during:*)
   "GERTRUDE".
CHOOSE A NICE SHADY SPOT,
FOR THE SUN'S SO HOT
THAT ITS RAYS YOU COULD GET CHARRED IN!

"Hamlet".
SHALL TAKE IN THE AIR,
PUT AWAY KINGLY CARE—
    "Gertrude". (*sits on bench*)
LAY YOUR HEAD IN MY LAP, DEAR!
HAVE A LITTLE NAP, DEAR!
    "Hamlet". (*pulls her to her feet, waves her toward arras*)
NO, GO AWAY!
I WOULD RATHER LAY
ON THE MARBLE BENCH SO COOLING!
will do so, lying on his right side—head not *going to benchtop,*
but staying at same angle perpendicular to the torso, like a
puppet's)
    "Gertrude".
VERY WELL, SUGARPLUM,
LET THE SWEET DREAMS COME!
GET YOUR MIND OFF ROYAL RULING!
    Both.
IT IS SWEET WHEN THE HEAT
JUST WON'T RETREAT,
TO LIE IN THE DAPPLED SHADE,
CONSENTING TO BE
CONTENT AND UNDISMAYED!
music interval [*brief; have players leg it!*] *during which*
    "GERTRUDE" will exit via arras and "CLAUDIUS"
    will peek from behind right column)
    "Claudius".
LONG HAVE I WAITED FOR THE
KING AT THIS RENDEZVOUS!
tiptoes down to stand over other man—whose eyes are
    now shut)
I SHALL MAKE THE THRONE
ALL MY VERY OWN—
NOT TO MENTION GERTRUDE, TOO!
NOW IS MY CHANCE TO POUR THE
POISON INTO HIS EAR!
does so, from small phial; "HAMLET" opens eyes, looks
    at him) NOW THE THRONE IS MINE!
    "Hamlet".
YOU'RE A FILTHY SWINE!
    "Claudius".
I'LL TAKE THE CROWN! (*whisks it from other man's head*)
THANKS A LOT! NOW LIE DOWN!

"HAMLET". (*while "CLAUDIUS" adjust crown on his own head*)
WOE IS ME! LACKADAY!
WHEN I HIT THE HAY,
WHAT HE DID WAS RATHER HEINOUS!
   "CLAUDIUS". (*finger-pressing against left temple of still neck rigid victim*)
THIS IS NO TIME TO CHAT!
YOU WILL SOON FALL FLAT!
POISON'S NOT LONG ON HUMANENESS!
(*"GERTRUDE" re-enters via arras, hastens to bench, on:*)
   "GERTRUDE".
WHAT IS THIS THAT I SEE?
THE MONARCHY
SEEMS READY TO TAKE A FALL!
   "HAMLET".
I FEAR I HAVE LOST MY LIFE, DEAR!
   "CLAUDIUS". (*embraces her*)
AND SO, WILL YOU BE MY WIFE, DEAR?
   "GERTRUDE".
THIS IS RATHER SUDDEN—
   "GERTRUDE/CLAUDIUS".
—BUT LOVE WILL BUD IN
NO TIME AT ALL!
   TRIO.
MELODRAMA FOR THREE
AS THE FAMILY TREE
GETS AN O- . . . VER- . . . HAUL!

(*on final beat of music [right after "-haul!"], "GERTRUDE" and "CLAUDIUS" do a quick in-tempo lip-peck kiss, as—on same beat— "HAMLET" lets his head drop sideways at last, eyes shut tight; song's over, but lights remain the same as we hear SPECTATORS APPLAUD [it is hoped your audience is doing the same]; then APPLAUSE DIES, and soon as the lull is low enough in volume, we hear:*)

CLAUDIUS. (*from throne in darkness, an agonized shriek:*) Lights! Give me lights! (*FULL LIGHTS UP onstage; CLAUDIUS is standing before his throne, his face contorted with emotion, ALL OTHERS looking at him; then, in chummy matter-of-fact voice, he continues:*) The Queen dropped her Milk Duds! (*picks up box, hands it to GERTRUDE*)

GERTRUDE. Thank you, dearest!

HAMLET. (*faces out front, makes that comic frustration/chagrin-gesture* [*both fists before chest, knees slightly bent, and shoulders raised to about half-shrug height — then, simultaneously, knees bend slightly more as shoulders drop to normal position and fists arrive before stomach; this is normally accompanied by a grunt, but in this case:*], *says:*) Drat!

MAJOR-DOMO. Show's over! Everybody back to the buffet! (*general exodus via various archways except for principals*)

CLAUDIUS. By the way, Hamlet, I've abruptly decided to send you to Britain! I'll give you the details later. Right now, I've got to write a letter of introduction.

(*CLAUDIUS and GERTRUDE will now exit via A, with PO-LONIUS right behind them — but at last moment* [*unnoticed by HAMLET or OPHELIA*], *POLONIUS will dodge from view behind arras*)

HAMLET. (*very glum*) Well — did you notice *anything* in the king's manner?

OPHELIA. Only his sudden urge to get you out of *town!* What's the Britain-bit, anyhow?

HAMLET. Search me. Probably one of those protocol-things or something. I could use the sea-voyage — maybe it'll clear my head.

OPHELIA. Well — *me* for that buffet-table before they run low on melon balls! Coming? (*heads toward B*)

HAMLET. Not just yet. I want to stay here and brood a little longer. (*he sits on bench, she exits via B during:*)

OPHELIA. Suit yourself, honey. (*she is gone; a moment later, GERTRUDE hurries in via A, sees him, comes up behind him, suddenly covers his eyes with her hands*)

GERTRUDE. Guess who!

HAMLET. Mother. I'd know that sweet voice among a million! (*as she uncovers his eyes and comes around to sit beside him:*) Besides, your hands smell like the king's after-shave!

GERTRUDE. Now, son, I *must* talk with you! Whatever have you done to upset your uncle the king so dreadfully?

HAMLET. (*with surprise — and slow elation*) *Have* I then upset him? I wonder — mayhap the thing worked *despite* the Bavarian clockmaker!

GERTRUDE. All I know is that he's mumbling under his breath, insisting that he wants you out of his sight for awhile, and is writing a letter right now for you to take to the King of England when you go!

HAMLET. That's a long, lonesome journey I must undertake.

GERTRUDE. Not so lonesome as all that — he is sending Rosie and Gilda with you — to make sure you *do* go to England, I suspect — for your conduct has been uncommon strange.

HAMLET. (*jumps to his feet*) Then I was *right*! The ghost spoke *true*! Mine uncle *did* murder my father!

GERTRUDE. What's that?! What dreadful tidings are you vouchsafing here? My husband — a murderer — of my *other* husband?!

HAMLET. (*pacing so that he'll eventually be near arras*) Dark things are afoot at Elsinore, Mother! I suggest that you avoid the king as much as possible, for his doom is now assured, and those in his vicinity might well be inadvertently dragged to that self-same doom *with* him!

GERTRUDE. *What*? You speak of murder — and your uncle's doom — and now you are saying that murderous doom does impend over *me* also?!

POLONIUS. (*behind arras*) Oh! The Queen is in danger! Help, somebody, help!

HAMLET. *Aha*! (*draws sword, stabs through flap of arras, withdraws sword*) *Dead* — for a *ducat*!

GERTRUDE. I don't have a ducat on me — but I might wager half a crown — ?

HAMLET. (*points toward arras*) Is it the *king*?

GERTRUDE. I think you mean, "*Was* it the king," considering!

HAMLET. (*looks at sword*) It *is* a pointy little thing, isn't it! (*re-sheathes it, then reaches for arras-flap*) Shall we have a look-see? (*peeks through flap, pauses, then comes out again*) Whoopsy!

GERTRUDE. Who is it?

HAMLET. Polonius. Ophelia is gonna be really *ticked* about this! (*takes GERTRUDE's arm, starts toward A*) You know, a long sea-voyage might be *just* the thing, considering!

(*as they exit via A, LIGHTS SHIFT to only G-H-I areas* [*during this upstage-blacking-out, POLONIUS can make his exit*], *and MUSIC INTROS, and — proceeding from C toward B — we have:*

ROSIE/GILDA.
HIS SENSES ARE SO SMITTEN

HE'S STUPID AS A KITTEN!
WE'LL GO WITH HIM TO BRITAIN
TILL HIS BRAIN BEGINS TO CLEAR!
IT'S EASY TO DISCERN HE
COULD USE A PLEASANT JOURNEY!
PERHAPS WHEN WE RETURN E-
VENTS WILL NOT BE SO SEVERE!

*(they are gone [via B]; LIGHTS UP FULL; a moment later,
LAERTES enters via C simultaneous with GERTRUDE entering via A; they will espy one another, and move to conjoin
just upstage of bench, during:)*

GERTRUDE. Laertes! Then you *did* get my message!

LAERTES. And did depart for Elsinore even from the very
midst of my classes on the subsequent tide! What terrible tragedy
is upon us! Thy son gone mad — my father most cruelly slain —
and I'm *sure* to flunk geometry!

GERTRUDE. *(takes his hands as they meet)* Mayhap you can
make it up in a summer session!

LAERTES. I do hope so! But to matters at hand: How sits this
sad circumstance with my sweet sister?

GERTRUDE. *(evasively)* Uh . . . everybody . . . deals with
tragedy . . . in their own manner . . . She has — how shall I
put it? — found a rather singular method of mourning dear de-
parted Polonius . . .

LAERTES. Marking thy manner, I do dread to hear't!

GERTRUDE. "Heert"?

LAERTES. *Hear* . . . *it.*

GERTRUDE. Oh.

LAERTES. And what method of mourning has my sweet sister
selected?

GERTRUDE. She does wander about the place from room to
room, carrying a small basket of herbs and flowers, wistfully
wafting her sorrow in snatches of song as she does bestow the
burden of her basket upon all and sundry!

LAERTES. Alas! Where wanders this afflicted maid, for I would
share with her my sorrow!

GERTRUDE. I do believe I hear her approaching even now!

*(and indeed she does; and so do we, as MUSIC INTROS, and
then OPHELIA — basket over her arm — enters via B at the
head of a conga-line of TROUPERS — their itinerary will be*

*across G-H-I area, up behind thrones, down in front of arras,
up around behind arras, then down past GERTRUDE and
LAERTES [who stand quietly and observe entire song],
around the left end of bench, and finally out again via B —
except that during final downstage cross toward B, OPHE-
LIA will disengage from front of conga-line and dance back-
wards slightly till she can pick up tail-end of line and thus be
the last one to dance offstage again; got that? Okay, then here
we go, with a most unmournful OPHELIA leading the line:)*

OPHELIA.
HERE'S ROSEMARY FOR REMEMBRANCE!
HERE'S PANSIES FOR THOUGHTS OF YOU!
I MOVE LIKE A GERBIL
WHOSE FEELINGS GROW VERBAL
TO DANCE TO AN HERBAL REVIEW!

IF YOU CANNOT SEE A SEMBLANCE
OF SENSE IN THE SONG I SING,
WHEN LIFE HAS GONE SOUR,
ONE SCOURS EACH BOWER
TO SHARE EV'RY FLOWERING THING!
TROUPERS.
IT'S PAINFUL WHEN YOUR LOVER
HAS MADE YOUR DADDY DEAD!
YOUR BRAIN GOES UNDERCOVER
AND OFTEN LEAVES YOUR HEAD!
OPHELIA.
THOUGH I BEAR A STRONG RESEMBLANCE
TO SOMEONE WHO'S NOT ALL THERE,
HOW CAN I CONTINUE?
I'D MUCH RATHER SPRINT TO
ENTWINE DAISIES INTO MY HAIR!
TROUPERS.
THERE'S JUST NO COMPENSATION
FOR BLASTED ROMANCE!
OPHELIA.
MY ONLY CONSOLATION
IS PASSING OUT THESE PLANTS!
WHEN YOUR LIFE'S INHUMAN,
TRY A LITTLE CUMIN!

TROUPERS.
SUBLIMATE YOUR GLOOM IN
VEGETATION!
  OPHELIA.
PEPPERMINT IS PERKY
WHEN EVENTS ARE MURKY!
  TROUPERS.
CORIANDER'S HER KEY
TO SEDATION!
  OPHELIA.
WHEN YOU'RE OFF YOUR BEAN—
  TROUPERS.
—GO FOR SOMETHING GREEN!
  OPHELIA/TROUPERS.
PHILOSOPHERS MAY CONDEMN PLANTS
AS USELESS FOR MISERY!
BUT JOY BY THE CARTON
IS THERE IN YOUR GARDEN,
SO WHY LEAVE YOUR HEART IN DEBRIS?
WHEN SUDDEN SORROWS INJURE
WITH PUNITIVE HELL,
JUST PLUCK A LITTLE GINGER
AND SOON YOU'LL BE WELL!
IF LIFE LEAVES YOU WEAK,
THINK OF CHIVES AND PAPRIK-
A, AND RE-
MEMBER ROSE- . . . MAR- . . . Y . . . ! (*they are
  gone; there is a silence; then:*)

LAERTES. Well, at least she's in good voice!
GERTRUDE. Yes, but the castle gardens are *such* a mess!

(*she takes his arm and they start up toward A, where they will exit
  in darkness, because already LIGHTING is only in G-H-I
  area, now, and ROSIE and GILDA enter via C, holding a
  large letter secured by an ostentatious royal seal; they will
  move gradually toward B, a few steps, then a pause, then
  repeat, etc., during their dialogue;*)

ROSIE. (*gazing about in awe*) So this is Buckingham Palace!
Kind of awesome!

GILDA. I have the oddest premonition we shouldn't have come here at all!

ROSIE. What *else* could we do? After those pirates sailed off with Prince Hamlet, *somebody* had to deliver this letter to the British monarch!

GILDA. I still don't like it! Did you see the size of that *pike* the guard back there was holding?

ROSIE. I was too busy looking at that big spear-and-axe combination he had!

GILDA. Rosie, that *is* a pike!

ROSIE. I thought a pike was a freshwater fish?

GILDA. Why would a palace guard carry a *fish*?

ROSIE. How *else* could it get around? (*when GILDA gives her an exasperated scowl:*) Can't swim on these marble floors . . .

GILDA. Now listen, Rosie—! (*but BOTH fall silent as haughty BUTLER enters via B*)

BUTLER. What are you commoners doing in Buckingham Palace?!

ROSIE. Please, sir, I'm Rosie Krantz and this is Gilda Stern— we've come to deliver a letter from King Claudius of Denmark.

GILDA. Are you impressed?

BUTLER. (*taking letter*) Hardly.

GILDA. Didn't think so.

BUTLER. You will wait here until I return from delivering this to His Majesty. (*turns and exits via B*)

ROSIE. We *will*?

GILDA. Boy, he's rude—didn't even *ask* us to wait. Are butlers supposed to give orders?

ROSIE. Search me. We're too poor to have servants. (*FOOT-MAN enters via C, starts cross toward B*)

GILDA. Hey there, fella—aren't there any *chairs* in this mausoleum?

FOOTMAN. (*stops*) I beg your pardon?

ROSIE. It's kind of hard on the feet standing around waiting.

FOOTMAN. And what, may I ask, are you waiting *for*?

GILDA. An answer to the letter we brought from King Claudius of Denmark!

FOOTMAN. (*reacts*) Good gracious, you *are* naive! Don't you know that that's the method kings use to get *rid* of people? Those letters always say to execute the bearer!

ROSIE. *Now* he tells us!

GILDA. *See*? My premonition was right! We've got to get *out* of here!

FOOTMAN. That's what *I'd* do! (*starts again toward B, they follow him almost to exit; he stops*) The exit, ladies, is the way you came *in* here! (*gestures toward C*)

ROSIE. But there's a big burly guard there carrying a barracuda!

GILDA. That's a *pike*!

ROSIE. Knew it was *something* dangerous!

FOOTMAN. Nonetheless, that is the *only* way out of here! (*turns and exits via B*)

GILDA. Say — I just realized — that letter — it must mean King Claudius was trying to get *Hamlet* bumped off!

ROSIE. But why take such terrible retribution against his own nephew?

GILDA. There's no time to puzzle it out *now* — let's get *out* of here!

(*MUSIC INTROS, and they will move* halfway *toward C, during:*)

BOTH.
WE'RE STUCK FOR A SOLUTION
TO HAMLET'S RETRIBUTION!
WE'RE DUE FOR EXECUTION
'CAUSE WE TRIED TO HELP A FRIEND!
(*at this point, with no break in music or tempo, they see a GUARD carrying a leveled pike* [not *the freshwater fish, please*] *coming toward them via C, so they reverse direction, and — GUARD moving at same pace as theirs — they will exit via B after finishing:*)
A FATE SO GRIM AND GORY
IS LESS THAN HUNKY-DORY!
IF THIS IS OUR LIFE STORY,
WHAT A ROTTEN WAY TO END!

(*they — and GUARD — are off; LIGHTS COME UP FULL; LAERTES enters via A just as GERTRUDE and ELSIN-ORITAS enter via C*)

GERTRUDE. Ah, Laertes! I fear I am the bearer of tragic tidings! (*ALL will eventually wind up in area upstage of bench, during:*)

LAERTES. You mean — I *did* flunk geometry?!

GERTRUDE. Oh, lots worse than that. I think . . . you had better sit down. (*indicates bench; he sits there, on upstage side, his back to us*)

LAERTES. Okay. I'm all braced. What *are* these tidings?

GERTRUDE. (*wringing her hands*) Oh, Laertes, your sister's drowned!

LAERTES. Oh no! Oh tragedy! Oh sorrow! How did it happen?

GERTRUDE. (*with ELSINORITAS in chorale formation behind her now*)

(MUSIC INTROS and she sings solemnly:)

OUT SEEKING FLOWERS UNTIL QUITE LATE,
SHE CLIMBED A TULIP TREE OUT BACK.
BUT SWEET OPHELIA WAS NO LIGHTWEIGHT,
AND SOFTLY THE BRANCH BEGAN TO CRACK!
AND . . . SHE . . . WENT . . .
(*MUSIC goes suddenly perky, and ELSINORITAS rock
   left and right, doing happy handclaps on the offbeat, during:*)

ALL BUT LAERTES.

DOWN, DOWN, DOWN THE RIVER WITH BILLOWS
   FOR PILLOWS!
HER GOWN, GOWN, GOWN THE WATERS DID
   DRINK AND SINK!
BUT STILL SHE SANG HER SILLY SONG
AS SHE FLOWED ALONG
TILL SHE RAN OUT OF BREATH
TO DROWN, DROWN, DROWN IN WATERY DEATH!
(*MUSIC goes solemn again for:*)

LAERTES. (*stands, approaches GERTRUDE to sing:*)
WHEN IN THE WATER YOU ESPIED HER,
WHILE FOR HER LIFE THERE WAS A HOPE,
WHY, FROM THE RIVERBANK BESIDE HER,
DID NOBODY THINK TO THROW A ROPE
WHEN . . . SHE . . . WENT . . .

ALL. (*perky again*)
DOWN, DOWN, DOWN THE RIVER, BOTH COATLESS
AND BOATLESS!
HER GOWN, GOWN, GOWN HER BODY DID TOW
   BELOW!

GERTRUDE.
THAT GAL WAS IN A SOGGY MESS—

LAERTES.
IN HER SOGGY DRESS—
ELSINORITAS.
AND HER SOGGINESS GREW—
ALL.
TILL DROWN, DROWN, DROWN WAS ALL SHE
COULD DO! (*solemn again:*)
GERTRUDE.
LAERTES, YOU MUST UNDERSTAND
I SELDOM HAVE A ROPE ON HAND!
I GUESS I COULD HAVE THROWN MY CROWN,
BUT THAT WOULD JUST HAVE WEIGHED HER DOWN!
LAERTES.
WAS NO OBSERVER THERE A SWIMMER?
GERTRUDE.
ONLY THE CAPTAIN OF THE GUARD.
LAERTES.
WHY FROM HER DOOM DID HE NOT SKIM HER?
GERTRUDE.
'CAUSE SWIMMING IN ARMOR'S RATHER HARD!
ALL.
SO . . . SHE . . . WENT . . .
(*perky again, this time with LAERTES and GERTRUDE
leading the handclapping ELSINORITAS in a dancing
parade about the stage*)
DOWN, DOWN, DOWN THE RIVER, PROVOKING A
SOAKING!
THAT GOWN, GOWN, GOWN WAS STARTING TO
GET QUITE WET!
BUT ONE COULD ONLY STAND AND SIGH
AS SHE WAFTED BY,
TILL SHE GURGLED FROM VIEW
TO DROWN, DROWN, DROWN WITH NEVER A
FROWN, FROWN, FROWN!
ELSINORITAS.
WE RECKON SHE'D GONE . . .
GERTRUDE.
HER ATTITUDE WAS CLEARLY WRONG!
ELSINORITAS.
. . . MAD . . .
LAERTES.
NOT MANY DROWNERS SING A SONG!

ALL.
AND IT'S INEXPRESSIBLY SAD!
OUR TEARS REVEAL THAT WE REALLY FEEL
BAD . . . ! *YEAH!*

GERTRUDE. We shall leave you now to nurture the nagging of your grievous grief! Come, ladies!

(GERTRUDE and ELSINORITAS exit via B; a moment later, CLAUDIUS peeks in via A, sees LAERTES alone, beckons to him; LIGHTS dim to illumine G-H-I area during:)

CLAUDIUS. *Pssst!*
LAERTES. Who, me?
CLAUDIUS. (*approaches him, keeping a wary eye out for GER-TRUDE*) I think you and I should have a little talk. Word has just reached me from England that my scheme to rid the world of Prince Hamlet has gone amiss, and that he shall be here again upon our shores momentarily.
LAERTES. You? His own uncle? Rid the world of him? Why?
CLAUDIUS. I have my reasons which shall remain mine own. But you, as the lad whose father perished upon Hamlet's sword-point, and whose sister was driven into madness and death by that father's loss at the hands of her belov-ed, should have no quarrel with my purpose, e'en though its cause remain mysterious.
LAERTES. That is so. If assist me in mine own vengeance you would, mine ears are thine to inform.
CLAUDIUS. (*takes him by the arm*) Then come with me, Laertes. We do have many matters to presently discuss.

(BOTH will exit via C; as they do so, LIGHTS COME UP to focus on bench-area [F] only, where we see that [during preceding dim-down] a fuzzy-grassy cloth [such as used to cover dirt-mounds at gravesides] has been cast over the bench, which now, under the cloth, represents such a dirt-mound covering; the unseen "grave" will be on the upstage side of the bench; to "get into" this grave, persons will simply get down upon their knees close to the upstage side; a moment after the lighting has been adjusted to this solitary area, HAMLET and HORATIO enter via A [if they are not immediately seen, they will enter into the upstage F-area within the next two speeches and be in full view])

HAMLET. I do thank thee, friend Horatio, for arranging my ransom from my pirate captors.

HORATIO. It took quite a hunk of change! I presume you will pay me back shortly?

HAMLET. So soon as the bank shall open on Monday next, I faithfully promise.

HORATIO. What ho! A fresh-dug grave — in the castle garden?

HAMLET. Like as not for *my* mortal remains, had the king's foul treachery succeeded. Luckily the letter indicated the death of the *bearer*, and did not mention me by name, or the minions of the British king might even now be seeking me out to fulfill mine uncle's fell fiat!

HORATIO. But your uncle must by now have learned of his scheme going askew — so why then dig this grave?

HAMLET. Perhaps he plots further toward my demise. We shall see! But look — what is this? (*springs down into grave, getting some object we do not yet see*) It is the skull of Yorick, the former court jester to Elsinore!

HORATIO. (*likewise getting into grave alongside HAMLET*) How can you be certain, milord?

HAMLET. There are some features that even tenure in a grave cannot efface! (*lifts Yorick's skull into view: It still wears a belled jester's cap and a ruff about its [unseen] neck; NOTE: This skull is a hand-puppet, whose jaws will shortly be operated by HAMLET, ostensibly simply supporting the skull on his hand; the "VOICE" of "Yorick" can be handled in one of three ways: 1) Have a HAMLET who is also a ventriloquist; 2) have an unseen CHORUS member lying from our view behind or beneath the bench to supply the voice; or 3) find a skull that can sing.*)

HORATIO. I see what you mean. Quite a comedown from the bubbly times at court!

HAMLET. (*nods wistfully*) Alas, poor Yorick! I knew him, Horatio. A fellow of infinite jest, of most excellent fancy; he has borne me on his back a thousand times; and now, how abhorred in my imagination it is! My gorge rises at it. Here hung those lips that I have kissed I know not how oft. Where be your gibes now? Your gambols? Your songs?

HORATIO. Ah, *sang* he then?

HAMLET. Incessantly. A voice more of dedication than mellifluity, I warrant, but his enthusiasm surpassed his talents, and we were all content to listen nonetheless. (*to "Yorick"*) Now get you to my lady's chamber, and tell her, let her paint an inch thick, to this favour must she come; make her laugh at *that!*

HORATIO. It *does* rather make all enterprise and ambition a goodly waste of time.

HAMLET. Indeed. One struggles, one strives, one hopes and labors—and for what? To arrive as a rotting mound of bones fit only to provoke incipient nausea!

(MUSIC INTROS, and he sings:)

IS THIS THEN OUR FINAL DESTINY?
IS LIFE BUT A FLUKE?
FOR THE MAN HE ONCE PROFESSED TO BE
I COULD TRULY PUKE!
   HORATIO.
A GRAVEYARD TENDS TO MAKE ME QUIVER, SIR;
STICK AROUND I CAN'T!
COME AWAY AND TRY SOME LIVERWURST
OR THE FRIED EGGPLANT!
(he starts to get out of grave, but BOTH freeze in panic when they see the skull's jaws move as:)
   YORICK. *(sings merrily)*
WON'T YOU STAY ON A LITTLE WHILE?
FOLKS SELDOM STEP IN!
   HORATIO. *(to HAMLET)*
TRY TO ACT NONCOMMITTAL WHILE
I FIND A WEAPON!
   HAMLET.
YORICK, AM I DREAMING?
   HORATIO.
OR SHOULD WE BOTH START SCREAMING?
   YORICK.
DON'T RUN AWAY! WON'T YOU STAY?
   HAMLET.
IT'S NOT EASY WHEN ONE'S QUEASY!
   YORICK.
BUT MY NEW LOCATION
IS SHORT ON CONVERSATION!
PLEASE DON'T REFUSE! WHAT'S THE NEWS?
   HAMLET.
DENMARK'S GOTTEN RATHER ROTTEN!
   HORATIO.
HOW CAN YOU SIT THERE
AND CHAT WITH DEAD YORICK'S HEAD?

HAMLET.
DOWN IN THE PIT, THERE,
I KNOW THAT I SOON MUST LIE!
    YORICK.
THAT'S THE TICKET! NOW, WHAT'S SO WICKED
THAT YOU ARE SICKENED AND SAD OF HEART?
    HORATIO. (*to HAMLET*)
STOP ENCOURAGING TOPICS FRIGHTENING!
DROP THAT AWFUL THING! LET'S DEPART!
(*HAMLET eagerly drops skull back into grave*)
    HAMLET/HORATIO. (*with great relief and slight embarrassment*)
HOW COULD WE
HAVE BEEN SO PANICKY?!
WHEN ONE'S MOOD GROWS CONVERSATIONAL
BY AN OPEN GRAVE,
SIMPLE MORBID FASCINATION'LL
MAKE BRAINS MISBEHAVE!
REFLECTING BY A COLD CADAVER IN
AMBIENCE OF DREAD,
(*they will get out of grave on next two lines, and as they do so, LIGHTING WILL COME UP FULL, being at top brightness by the time they are standing upstage of "grave"*)
YOU MAY FIND YOURSELF PALAVERIN'
WITH A CORPSE'S HEAD!
    HORATIO.
THUS NIGHTFALL MAKETH MEN HALLUCINATE!
    HAMLET. (*gives him light nudge with elbow*)
AIDED BY THAT CHARLOTTE RUSSE YOU ATE!

    BOTH.
'TIS MERE MESMERIZING BY THE MOON . . . !
    YORICK.
(*voice hollow, from open grave before them*)
BUT COME BACK SOON . . . !

(*BOTH react, panic, and start backward toward the A-exit keeping a wary eye on that open grave all the while, moving in tempo to play-out of song — then leap from view offstage on final note of song; a moment later, GRAVEDIGGER enters via B, carrying shovel, moves to forefront of bench, and at that moment, HAMLET and HORATIO peek back in at A, re-*

gain courage on seeing the man at gravesite, and re-enter, moving down to F during:)

HAMLET. Ho there, Gravedigger!

GRAVEDIGGER. Why, 'tis young Prince Hamlet! Glad I am to see you, milord! I'd heard it given out you were pirate-kidnapped en route to England, and I'd thought ne'er upon you again to lay mine eyes!

HORATIO. But — if you thought *that* — then for whom *are* you digging yon grave?

GRAVEDIGGER. Why, for the last mortal traces of that fair and most lamented maiden Ophelia!

HAMLET. (*shrieks*) Ophelia's grave?! No! I won't believe it! It cannot be!

HORATIO. Why not, milord?

HAMLET. (*matter-of-factly. pointing at "grave"*) Well, for *one* thing, it's not *wide* enough!

GRAVEDIGGER. Oh, but 'twill serve, Prince Hamlet — her sweet body was never recovered from the waters in which she drowned. We do but bury her silken scarf found at riverside, in symbolic token of her sodden passage.

HAMLET. Alas, alas, alas! This is all *my* doing, Horatio, ill-starred product of my feckless quest for vengeance! Do I here and now *renounce* that evil ambition! Live and let live! No more shall I a vile avenger be! Wilt help me in this endeavor, friend Horatio?

HORATIO. I most certainly wilt! (*takes his arm*) Come on, let's find us some *chow*! Ransoming always makes me ravenous!

(*they will exit via A: LIGHTS DIM DOWN to illuminate only G-H-I area, during which time GRAVEDIGGER will clear green bench-cover and "Yorick" [and if you have a hidden Yorick-voice person hidden there, he too should depart at this time], and also exit via A; but as soon as lighting in G-H-I is established, CLAUDIUS will enter via B, almost simultaneous with ROSIE and GILDA entering via C; ALL stop on seeing opposite entrants, then will slowly converge in H-area during:*)

CLAUDIUS. Ah! My trusted emissaries! Bring you news of Prince Hamlet's jaunt to England in your caretaking company?

ROSIE. For starters, he never *got* there!

GILDA. Our ship was attacked by pirates, there was a fight, in the fight he boarded the pirate ship —

ROSIE. —and suddenly the ships parted as the pirates began to take the worse of the battle—

BOTH. —so sailed we on to England alone!

CLAUDIUS. (*who's been trying vainly to get a word in*) Of all *that* am I already aware! It is the young prince's present whereabouts of which I wish to wot!

BOTH. To *what*?

CLAUDIUS. Not "what"—"*wot*"! To *know* about! I have heard he has been ransomed, and shall certainly head for *here*—I had hoped you could more closely inform me *when*!

ROSIE. For me, the sooner the better!

GILDA. Thanks to you and your treacherous letter!

ROSIE. Calling down death on the bearer!

GILDA. But luckily handled in error!

CLAUDIUS. What are you talking about? What error?

GILDA. We did deliver your letter by the proxy of the English king's snobbish butler.

ROSIE. And 'twas *he* thus put to instant death!

GILDA. We would have returned here sooner—

ROSIE. —but we tarried to cheer at the butler's execution!

BOTH. Now if you'll excuse us—you stinker!—we're gonna whoop it up at the punchbowl! (*they exit via B; CLAUDIUS remains in H-area, wringing his hands*)

CLAUDIUS. O most dreadful dread of impending doom! If they should inform the Queen that I conspired against the life of her royal offspring—! (*looks left as LAERTES hurries in via B*) Well, it's about *time*! We have matters of great moment to discuss!

LAERTES. Sorry, sire. You wouldn't *believe* the long line for the bathroom! That potent punch is a real kick in the kidneys! Now, about this revenge-thing—I'm as brave as the next man, you understand—but I do fear the consequence of killing the heir to the throne of Denmark!

CLAUDIUS. Thou'lt have a king for thy protector! Be secure and fear naught!

LAERTES. And if the *Queen* finds out—?

CLAUDIUS. Don't *say* things like that! If we do it aright, suspicion shall not fall upon us! I hope.

LAERTES. Yet a frosty fear does increasingly cool mine ardor for avengement!

CLAUDIUS. Then must thou rekindle its flame apace! What other course lies open to thine honor? (*MUSIC INTROS, and he sings:*)

NOW THAT HAMLET HAS SLAIN THY FATHER,
AND OPHELIA'S INTERRED,
WHAT DO YOU PLAN TO DO?
(*a very ill-at-ease LAERTES reluctantly nods as he joins
    in song:*)
   BOTH.
THERE'S BUT ONE THING TO
PLAN: LET'S GET HIM!
   LAERTES.
I COULD SLAY HIM WITHOUT MUCH BOTHER,
BUT IF ANYONE HEARD,
'TWOULD BE THE DEATH OF ME!
(*he and CLAUDIUS will staunchly handshake, holding the
    clasp for the next two lines of the song:*)
   BOTH.
STILL AND ALL, IF WE
CAN, LET'S GET HIM!

THERE MUST BE SOME METHOD MERITORIOUS
WHENCE TO BRING ABOUT HIS FINAL BREATH!
VENGEANCE IF WE GOT IT WOULD BE GLORIOUS,
BUT NOT IF IT MEANT
WE TWO WOULD BE SENT
TO PRISON AND DEATH!
   CLAUDIUS.
HAMLET'S PROUD OF HIS SKILL AT FENCING!
I'VE HEARD YOU ARE GOOD, TOO!
IF I ARRANGED A MATCH—
   BOTH.
—THAT COULD SOON DISPATCH
HIM FOREVER!
   LAERTES.
ALSO, JUST TO ENSURE DISPENSING
HIM, THE POINT I'LL IMBUE
WITH VENOM SUBTLE, TILL—
   BOTH.
—JUST ONE CUT'LL KILL
HIM! HOW CLEVER!
   CLAUDIUS.
AND AS A PRECAUTION I WILL DROP A RING
POISON-LADEN IN THE WINNER'S CUP!
   LAERTES.
THAT WAY, IF I LOST IT WOULDN'T HURT A THING!

BOTH.
HOW CLEVER THE TRAP!
WHICHEVER MAY HAP,
HIS NUMBER IS UP!

LET US HASTEN TO START THINGS MOVING!
CLAUDIUS.
I'LL GO POISON THAT RING!
LAERTES.
AND I'LL INFECT THE BLADE!
BOTH.
THEN WE'VE GOT IT MADE!
HAMLET'S HAD IT!
THOUGH I HOPE IT'S DUE TO ME
THE COFFIN WILL SLAM, YET
EITHER WAY WE'RE GONNA SEE
THE END OF PRINCE HAMLET!
HIS EXISTENCE MUSTN'T ENDURE!
LET'S GET HIM FOR SURE . . . !
(*they will exit via B during play-off music, and just before
    they vanish from view will shout:*)
YEAH!

(*The moment they are off, HORATIO — with large tray of food
  — will enter via A, humming happily, moving down toward C; just
    about the time he reaches I-area, OPHELIA pops in via C;
    she wears sneakers, dungarees, a sailor's knit-cap, and a
    large sweatshirt on the breast of which is printed: "ROYAL
    DANISH COAST GUARD"*)

OPHELIA. Hiii!
HORATIO. (*nearly drops tray*) Ophelia! You're *alive*! But—
they buried your silken scarf this very morning!
OPHELIA. Good thing I wasn't *wearing* it!
HORATIO. But the Queen saw you drown!
OPHELIA. I just ducked underwater to get out of my soggy
clothes— they were dragging me down something fierce! When I
came up again, I was floating out to sea in my undies! Luckily,
some people on the shore informed the coast guard, and they sent
a boat after me!
HORATIO. Some people saw *you* in the sea and called the coast
guard? *What* people?

OPHELIA. Some group called *Save The Whales*! . . . Should I resent that?!

HORATIO. Ah, what matter! We must hasten to tell Prince Hamlet of your survival!

OPHELIA. No-no! Not a word. I want to *surprise* him!

HORATIO. You sure you won't *shock* him into a *coronary*? And your brother as well?

OPHELIA. Laertes? What's he doing here? Playing hookey again? I *told* him I'd tutor him in geometry if things got too tough!

HORATIO. Alas, he came home for your father's funeral — and stayed on for your own.

OPHELIA. (*starts toward B*) Well, not a word to *anybody*, please! Not till I've had something to eat. Swimming in the North Sea gives me an appetite!

(she exits via B an instant before HAMLET enters via A, toting a
trayful of food as large as HORATIO's)

HAMLET. What, not in the garden yet? I told thee to save me a place at thy table!

HORATIO. Well, you see, milord — (*but BOTH cease speaking as OSRIC, a dandily foppish man, enters via C*)

OSRIC. Ah, your highness! I do bring you a message from the king!

HAMLET. And who might *you* be?

OSRIC. Osric.

HORATIO. Hello. Ah's Horatio!

HAMLET. And ah's Hamlet! Glad to meet you, Rick!

OSRIC. No, it all's one word!

HAMLET. Know-it-all is *three* words!

HORATIO. With two hyphens.

OSRIC. Are you guys funning me — ?

HAMLET. Bear with our playfulness, kind Osric. We do but jest to celebrate the wearisome weight so recently lifted from my heart. What message sends the king?

OSRIC. His majesty would have you entertain the court with an exhibition of fencing, to be between you and that most accomplished swordsman young Laertes.

HORATIO. Milord, I like this not.

HAMLET. What harm can there be in it, Horatio? And even if harm there be, to what avail does a man seek to evade his determined destiny? After all, if it be now, 'tis not to come; if it be not to come, it will be now; if it be not now, yet it will come: The readiness is all!

OSRIC/HORATIO. (*stare at him for one beat; then, in confused unison:*)Hah—?

HAMLET. Forget it. Come, Horatio, let us rid ourselves of this provender betimes; I fence better when my stomach is not filled to repletion. (*they start off via C*)

OSRIC. And what shall I then tell the king?

HAMLET. Yes. Tell him yes. By all means, yes.

OSRIC. (*as they exit via C*) Very well, your highness! (*turns slightly upstage, cups his hands about his mouth and shouts:*) HEY KING!

CLAUDIUS. (*off*) WHAT?

OSRIC. *THE SWORDFIGHT IS ON!*

CLAUDIUS. (*off*) *Super!* Come on, Gert, it's showtime!

MAJOR-DOMO. (*off*) Make way for his majesty the king!

(*and we do the FANFARONADE bit all over again: MUSIC . . . Major-Domo's "His Majesty the king! . . . MUSIC BUILDUP . . . CLAUDIUS's "All right, already! I'm here, I'm here!" . . . and unsuitable JAZZY FINISH to MUSIC; then:*)

CLAUDIUS. But where is our young prince?

HAMLET. (*enters via C, HORATIO with him, both minus trays now*) At thy beck and call, my uncle the king!

OSRIC. (*carrying velvet cloth supporting weapons*) And here be the swords!

LAERTES. Shall I have first choice?

HAMLET. As the challenger, that is thy privilege, good Laertes.

(*NOTE: Player-setup is this: GERTRUDE/CLAUDIUS will remain standing before their thrones; CHORUS will crowd downstage below edge of bench, but leaving sightlines so we can still see the thrones; HAMLET/LAERTES will fence in the G-H-I area; each time fencing starts, G-H-I area will remain FULL BRIGHT; but rest of stage at least HALF FULL BRIGHT; lighting will come up FULL at the climax of all three encounters, and remain fully bright for remainder of play after final encounter*)

CLAUDIUS. And I into this goblet shall drop this precious ring, so that the drink and the ring shall be the prize of he who scores on the first pass!

GERTRUDE. *What* ring?

CLAUDIUS. (*looks at his bare finger*) Drat! It must be still back upon my dressing-table!

HORATIO. Stand fast, milord king! I shall fetch it for thee forthwith! (*will rush upstage and exit via A, during:*) And that's not easy to say with a mouthful of melon balls!

HAMLET. Shall we begin or nay?

OSRIC. Oh, don't begin; I'd rather hear you neigh!

HAMLET. Getting cutesy?

OSRIC. Sorry, milord.

LAERTES. (*already a nervous basket-case with dread*) Let us begin at once!

CLAUDIUS. (*quickly, lest LAERTES' uneasiness cause comment*) Yes, at once! I do ordain it! Places! Begin!

HAMLET. *En garde!*

LAERTES. *En garde!*

(*HAVE AT THEE* NOW! *instrumental is played by accompanist, ending with HAMLET "pinking" LAERTES over the heart with his foil on final chord, and CHORUS shouting on final followup filagree:*)

CHORUS. A palpable hit!

LAERTES. (*observing with relief*) Thou strikest hard, milord! Fortunate for me thy foil has a *button* at its end!

HAMLET. Be not so yet reliev-ed, Laertes—hast never had a foil-button up thy *nose?* (*LAERTES reacts with fingers to nose*) See thou guard thy nostrils well!

LAERTES. (*annoyed at his own cowardice*) Have at thee again!

HAMLET. As thou wilt! *En garde!*

LAERTES. *En garde!*

(*as before, they cross sword-tips, fence carefully for a brief spell as each takes the measure of the other's ability, then go faster and faster, until—in almost* identical *choreography—HAMLET once again "pinks" LAERTES over the heart on final chord, and, again on final musical filagree:*)

CHORUS. A palpable hit!

HORATIO. (*rushing in via A*) Your ring, your majesty!

CLAUDIUS. (*takes it*) Our thanks, Horatio! (*drops ring into goblet*) Hamlet, our son — come drink of thy reward! (*extends cup; HAMLET moves up to take it*)

GERTRUDE. (*grabs cup*) No, 'twould be bad for thy wind! Here, dab that sweating brow with my kerchief, Hamlet, and do thou then go back to thine exciting exhibition!

HAMLET. (*does so*) I thank thee, Mother!

(LAERTES, meanwhile, sags in dismay at the non-drinking by HAMLET, looks to CLAUDIUS, who gives a helpless shrug of his own frustration; trembling, LAERTES makes his decision, and as HAMLET turns from wiping his brow, lunges at him, nicking his arm [see PRODUCTION NOTES] with the swordtip; ALL OTHERS gasp; this lunge occurs on LAERTES' desperately shouted line:)

LAERTES. Have at thee *now*!

HAMLET. (*looks from bloodied arm to the point of LAERTES's foil, and:*) As thou wilt. (*and with a quick one-two-three of his foil, has LAERTES's sword down, picks it up, hands LAERTES the harmless foil in exchange; LAERTES, in terror, backs down into H-area, during:*) What, no more stomach for fighting? Why, I have scarce begun!

CLAUDIUS. (*desperately*) Part them, they're incensed!

OSRIC. (*does double-take*) Who, *me*?

(then final HAVE AT THEE NOW! instrumental starts; this time, the MUSIC is fierce, frightening, and just as HAMLET lunges with the sword toward LAERTES' breast, OPHELIA [still in rescue-clothing] bursts out of forefront of CHORUS to intercede, arms outstretched, her back to LAERTES, on:)

OPHELIA. "*SURPRIIISE!*"

(but it's too late; HAMLET's sword plunges into her stomach [see PRODUCTION NOTES]; a shocked LAERTES steps forward, embracing her from behind, his face cheek to cheek with hers [he's on the downstage side, face-wise], and MUSIC PAUSES; then HAMLET, seeing the position LAERTES is in, plunges the sword even farther through OPHELIA and — we can tell by his shocked expression — LAERTES, too, is impaled, on final chord of MUSIC; after a frozen moment, HAMLET pulls his sword back a bit, and

LAERTES slides to the floor; then pulls it out all the way, and OPHELIA slides to the floor; after about two beats of silence:)

HAMLET. Whoopsy!

OPHELIA. (*holding bloody stomach*) *Boy*, that smarts!

HAMLET. A doctor! Call a doctor!

GERTRUDE. Oh, this is dreadful! (*raises cup to her lips*)

CLAUDIUS. Gertrude, do not drink!

GERTRUDE. (*as if there were no comma in his cry, answers playfully:*) Oh, of *course* she do! (*drinks, reacts, drops cup*) *Aaagh!* I am poisoned! (*drops back onto throne, clutching throat*)

CLAUDIUS. Nonsense! She but swoons to see them bleed! (*wipes with one hand against his shirt, looks down at it*) *Why* is my hand all wet?

HORATIO. Oh, *my* fault, sire! On the way back, I stopped for a snack, and the ring fell into the punchbowl!

ALL OTHERS. The *punchbowl?!* (*ALL but HAMLET, HORATIO, LAERTES and OPHELIA clutch throats*)

HAMLET. Glad *I* wasn't thirsty!

LAERTES. Ah, but you're *just* as bad off, Hammy! That swordpoint had enough venom on it to wipe out an army!

OPHELIA. Well, thanks a *lot*, Laertes!

HORATIO. (*first two words sounded as if they were "Good grief":*) Good *night*, sweet prince! How do you feel?

HAMLET. (*since ALL onstage but HORATIO are now variously staggering, swaying*) Never mind about me—what *I'm* curious about is—how do *you* feel?

HORATIO. Never better, milord!

CLAUDIUS. But the punch—the poisoned ring—?!

HORATIO. Didn't *have* any punch. I mean, after all, why make a *pig* of myself?

HAMLET. (*sagging to sit on bench, gradually reclining*) Are you saying the entire court of Denmark has been done in by a *freeloader?*

GERTRUDE. Kind of looks that way, doesn't it!

HAMLET. Horatio, if I weren't cashing in my chips, there are things I could tell you—but stay—enough—I only wish I were strong enough to spit into thine eye! (*sags, dies, and then so does everybody else, except:*)

HORATIO. And the rest . . . is *silence!*

OPHELIA. (*lifts head*) Not in a *musical*, you fathead!

(*MUSIC INTROS, and THE SLAIN will all get slowly to their feet, one by one, as they — starting very softly — sing:*)

ALL. (*including HORATIO*)
CORPSES HERE AND CORPSES THERE!
DENMARK'S THRONE'S A VACANT CHAIR!
THERE'S NOBODY LEFT TO CARRY ON!
(*a bit louder, ALL moving down toward stage lip
   [principals in center, please] as they continue:*)
GOODNIGHT, PRINCE! THE SLATE'S WIPED CLEAN!
FAREWELL, KING, AND GOODBYE, QUEEN!
HIGHBORN, LOW, AND IN-BETWEEN ARE GONE!

SINCE THAT EFFERVESCIN'
POISON SEALED OUR FATE,
WE'VE ALL LEARNED OUR LESSON
JUST A WEE BIT LATE!
(*MUSIC loudens, key shifts to higher pitch, and ALL now
   sing at peak volume of their voices, with pep and energy:*)
STRANGE EVENTS HAVE COME TO PASS
HERE AMONG THE RULING CLASS.
ELSINORE'S AN EMPTY CASTLE NOW!
THIS IS HOW OUR STORY ENDS:
LIFELESS FOES AND FALLEN FRIENDS.
BUT TRADITION RECOMMENDS WE BOW!
(*ALL will do a slow unified bow, during:*)
SO PLEASE APPLAUD AS WE KOW-TOW . . . !
(*they reach full bow, now, and hold position as —*)

THE CURTAIN FALLS

- End of Show -

PRODUCTION NOTES

1) THE DUEL: First off, *all* swords should be blunt and safe; even make-believe dueling is dangerous. Now, as to LAERTES' sword (the one HAMLET will finally be using): It should have a telescoping blade; if you cannot find such a sword in a prop shop, make one from one of those telescoping blackboard-pointers used by teachers, which reduce to fountain-pen size for pocketing, and which have a safely blunt tip-button. Thus, when HAMLET impales OPHELIA (about a six-inch-deep stab) she will *immediately* clutch her stomach with both hands in apparent shock (actually, to hand-anchor that tip against her); then, his additional stab (about another six inches) into LAERTES merely telescopes the "sword" even more; finally, when he "withdraws the blade," OPHELIA must hang onto that tip so that the gadget can *un*-telescope to its full length as LAERTES and then OPHELIA fall to the floor. As for the "blood," simply have HAMLET, OPHELIA and LAERTES equipped with a small gelatin capsule filled with a suitably red stain (Disappearing Red Ink saves a lot of costume-cleaning — it only persists till it dries) to *crush* against the "wound" — HAMLET's arm, OPHELIA's stomach and (as he slides to the floor — his first opportunity to crush the capsule) LAERTES' stomach; The result is admirably startling and gory fun to see, audience-wise.

2) ODDS AND ENDS: If all the in-character bits of additional business that occurred to your author while writing this show were placed into the script, it would be as thick as the *complete* works of William Shakespeare; a few suggestions will show you the sort of thing that can augment/emphasize the comedic aspects of this play at various moments: For instance, in the opening number of the show, Gertrude could be carrying a bridal bouquet that she tosses merrily at the song's ending — to be caught by aged POLONIUS, causing laughter among all COURT members — which he can then "hand off" to the nearest CHORUS member in embarrassed disgruntlement . . . or when the Queen offers HAMLET her kerchief to wipe his brow, it can be balled up and obviously *used*, and stuck-together, and his followup-line can be altered to "*No* thank you, Mother!" just before LAERTES gives him that arm-stab . . . or when OPHELIA falls after the stabbing, she can go flat on her back with her legs (knees slightly bent) up in the air, and hold them thus, making her "death" somewhat less than poignant to view . . . or you can have ALL (Excepting HAMLET, HORATIO, GER-

TRUDE, LAERTES and OPHELIA) *holding* cups of punch in the final scene, and when CLAUDIUS says, "Hamlet, our son — come drink of thy reward!", ALL can "toast" HAMLET with a gesture and *drink* — thus setting up their horrified reaction to the announcement of poison-in-the-punchbowl even more so . . . or when POLONIUS gets stabbed, and HAMLET says "Shall we have a look-see?" (*if* your arras is the pull-cord type that can open centrally like tie-back drapes), have HAMLET pull the cord, revealing POLONIUS (not unlike the last remains of Obi-Wan Kenobi in *Star Wars*) as only a pair of sandals and a collapsed robe, at which sight HAMLET can remark, "It's PO-LONIUS! . . . I guess he really *was* an old windbag!", and then he can drop the pullcord and as drapes close again, go right to his "Ophelia is gonna be really *ticked* about this!" and continue as in the script with his next line and his-and-GERTRUDE's exit. In other words, you can *embellish* the events/moments in this show for even higher hilarity with just a bit of imaginative inventiveness here, there and elsewhere, so long as you remain within the important confines of what the characters and the story-line are about.

3) CAUTION: Paradoxically, since this is a comedy, it should be "played *straight*" for maximum audience-laughter; mugging, winking, and clowning will make the show *less* funny, not more. Each character *must* maintain his/her complete Earnestness Of Purpose at all times (except when the *script itself* indicates a deliberate out-of-character thing such as HAMLET's "*Ach Du Lieber!*"); that is, we need HAMLET to be fiercely moody and frustrated, OPHELIA to be lovelorn but sharp-witted, HORA-TIO to be almost *oblivious* to anything but the free lunch, GER-TRUDE to show guilt and motherly dismay, CLAUDIUS to reflect villainy and terror, LAERTES to convey an attitude both vengeful and fearful, etc., as deeply sincere and purposeful as they can. The straighter they play their roles, the louder the audience will laugh. But if they "try to *act* funny" they *won't* be. Trust the material; the script will do the work *for* you, laughter-wise; just remember that if you try to *look* funny, it makes the audience think you don't believe the script *itself* is funny — and then *they* won't think so. So follow the script, relax, and your audience will howl throughout. Trust me.

MONK FERRIS

Stage Setting

A, B & C: Archways/Entrances, D & E: Raised Platforms [appr. 8″ high], F: Stone Bench [appr. 18″ high, 2′ × 6′ top surface], On "D": 2 tall columns supporting arras [curtain], On "E": King's [K] and Queen's [Q] Thrones, G, H & I: Specific Playing Areas

[NOTE: If CHORUS is large, have additional archways in *side* (*Not* Upstage) walls of D & E platforms]

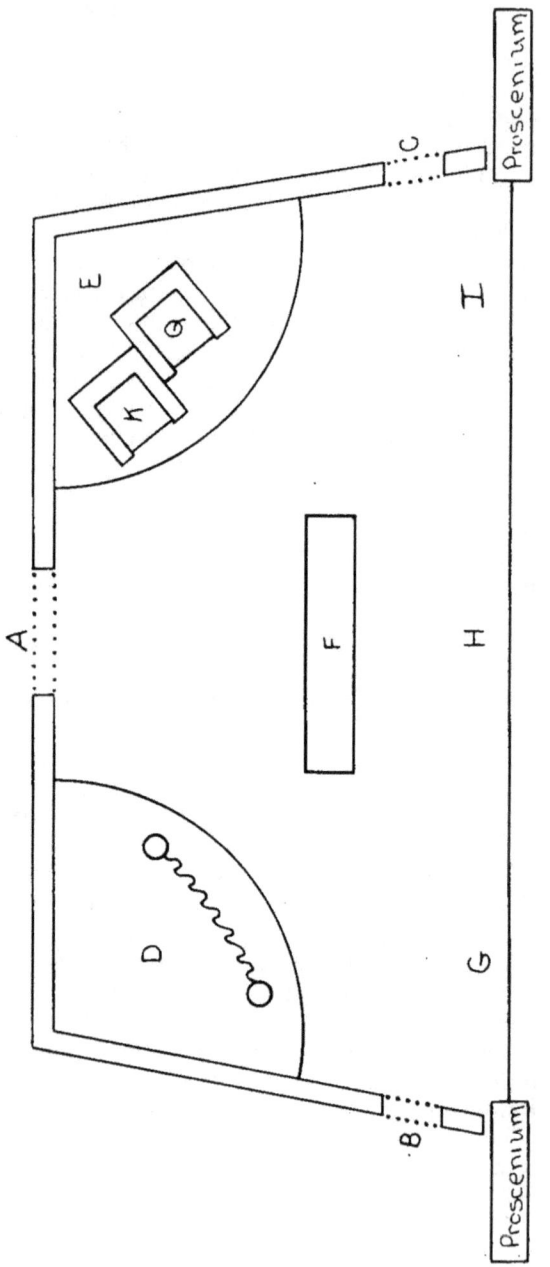